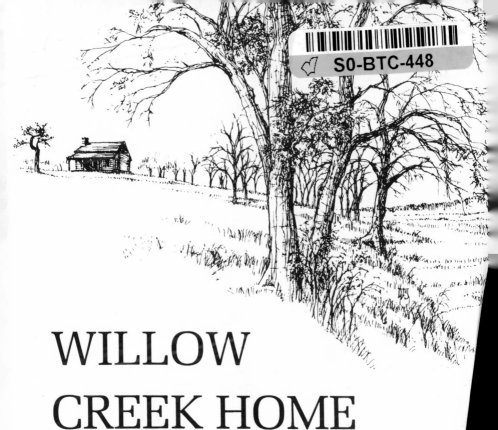

WILLOW
CREEK HOME

Janice Jordan Shefelman

Illustrated by
Tom • Karl • Dan
Shefelman

Eakin Press • Austin, Te

FIRST EDITION

Published in the United States of America
By Eakin Press
A Division of Sunbelt Media, Inc.
P.O. Box 90159
Austin, TX 78709

2 3 4 5 6 7 8 9

ISBN 0-89015-637-9

Library of Congress Catologing-in-Publication Data

hefelman, Janice Jordan, 1930-
  Willow Creek Home.

  ummary: A summer drought and epidemic illness in 1847 force Mina, Papa, and his
  wife, Lisette, to move on to a larger land grant deep in Comanche territory. Sequel
  \ Paradise Called Texas."
  Frontier and pioneer life—Fiction. 2. Texas—Fiction] I. Title.
  54115Wi 1985
)-89015-637-9

                                                          85-16189
                                                          CIP

as

For my one and only
Tom

AUTHOR'S NOTE

In *A Paradise Called Texas* Papa, Mama, and Mina left their ancestral home and village in Germany to come to Texas. It had been called "the paradise of North America" by the *Adelsverein,* a society of German nobles who were promoting a German colony in Texas. But instead of a paradise, the Jordans found sorrow, hardship, and adventure. Mama lay buried on that lonely Texas beach. Mina and Papa struggled inland and made a new home for themselves in the colony of Fredericksburg. Here they found *Tante* Lisette who became Mina's new mother and Papa's wife. In *Willow Creek Home,* drought and epidemic drive them on and on into Comanche territory.

Mina is a combination of two real life girls, and her story is based on the experiences of my German ancestors when they immigrated to Texas. The first Mina died during an epidemic in New Braunfels some six months after arriving in Texas. Her father, my great-grandfather, named his second daughter Mina to ease his grief. I think he would be happy that his beloved *kleine* Mina lives on in my stories.

Although some of the incidents in this book really happened, my fictional Mina is a girl who loves adventure, and she thought of other adventures that *could* have happened.

CONTENTS

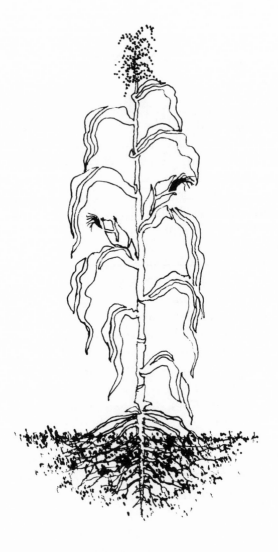

Dem Ersten Tod, dem Zweiten Not, dem Dritten Brot.

For the first generation, death; for the second, deprivation; for the third, bread.

1

NEWS

"What will we do, Papa, when there is nothing more to eat?"

Papa stopped as Mina examined the pitiful ear of corn. She pulled the husk away, but instead of juicy, plump kernels, the corn was dry and shrunk to the cob.

Mina looked up at Papa. There was a look in his eyes that told Mina he had been wondering the same thing. His broad kindly face was framed with a fringe beard. He was thinner than when they left Germany two years ago to come to Texas. He had a distracted look she had seen before — when Mama was sick.

"Something, *kleine* Mina," was all he said, nodding his head slowly and pressing his wide mouth shut into a thin hard line.

He had called her *kleine* Mina for all of her twelve years. Her real name was Johanne Ernestine Wilhelmine Jordan, but she was called Mina for short.

It was early morning, and already the Texas sun bore down on them, promising another day of heat and drought. The dry cornstalks rustled, and grasshoppers flew up before them as they walked along looking from side to side for corn.

Mina wondered what "something" might be. For a week they had eaten nothing but acorn bread. Even poor Liesel, the cow, had less milk to give. It was frightening to think about nothing more to eat. At night when she was alone up in the loft things seemed even worse. She wondered what it was like to starve to death, and imagined herself shrinking thinner until she was dried up like the ear of corn.

All that summer of 1847 there had been no rain in Fredericksburg, and the temperature soared to over one hundred degrees. Even the wild game had moved on to better grazing. Mina's friends, Chief Custaleta and his daughter Amaya, along with the whole tribe of Lipan Indians, had left their camp on the banks of the Pedernales to follow the wild animals. Only the German settlers remained — those who did not sicken and die of cholera.

The sun was making her head hurt. "Papa, let's go back to the cabin. There is no more corn to pick."

As they started silently for home someone came walking toward them from the other side of the cornfield with long lanky strides. It was *Herr* Kaufmann.

He waved to them. "Ernst, I have news," he shouted.

Mina was grateful for anything to break the spell of hopelessness she felt in that field of dead cornstalks. "Maybe it's good news, Papa." She looked up at him, hoping he would be cheered by that prospect.

"Ernst!" *Herr* Kaufmann shouted again. "The *Verein* has food supplies in New Braunfels. Johann Bader has been there and says the storehouse is full."

Papa quickened his pace, and they hurried toward *Herr* Kaufmann. He was a slim, elegant man, strangely out of place in a cornfield. He would look more at home in a lady's parlor, sipping tea from a china cup.

"You say there are food supplies?"

"*Ja*, Ernst."

"Then why haven't they sent our share to us?"

"That's a good question. Johann says they are trying to keep it all for themselves, and not let us know. He saw with his own eyes — supplies stacked to the roof — corn, potatoes, even wheat flour and coffee!"

Papa's eyes sharpened, and a renewed spirit seemed to take hold of him.

"By heaven, Heinrich, I'll not stand by and watch my family grow weaker by the day, while they fill their stomachs in New Braunfels." Papa pounded a fist into the palm of his hand.

"I feel the same way, Ernst, but what can we do?"

Papa thought a moment, his lips clamped together. Then he continued. "If they won't send the food, then we must get it ourselves, even if we have to fight."

Fight! Mina could not imagine her gentle Papa fighting. He had never struck anyone or anything. Now his eyes looked fierce — determined. Maybe this was the "something" Papa said he would do.

"Let's meet at my cabin this evening and decide on a plan," Papa said.

"Very well, Ernst. I'll talk to Johann and some others. You talk to Emil Hessler."

2

SEVEN MEN WITH CLUBS

That evening *Herr* Kaufmann came with five other men. Counting Papa there were seven in all. Some sat on the rough bench in front of the Jordan's cabin, others stood talking together.

Mina sat on a barrel beside the front door, and flicked her blonde braids back over her shoulders as she watched the men. She swung her bare feet back and forth, thumping the barrel.

Tante Lisette, Mina's new mother, stood in the doorway with her apron tied over her enlarged waist. The men had all paid their respects to Lisette, and were especially kind, because a woman with child is an object of honor — almost as though she held baby Jesus within her womb. Mina thought her face did look more beautiful than ever, even angelic. Lisette smoothed the dark strands of hair that had escaped the coiled braid at the back of her neck.

"Let's get on with the business at hand," Papa suggested, and the group fell silent. "I propose that we take

4

matters into our own hands, and go to New Braunfels to get our food."

"I agree," said *Herr* Bader.

"*Ja,* I'm ready, Ernst," said Emil Hessler, "but what if the *Verein* refuses to give us the supplies?"

"Then we will fight," said another as he stood shaking his clenched fist.

"What! With our bare hands? They will outnumber us."

"Are you suggesting guns?"

"*Jawohl!*" It was *Herr* Bader.

"*Nein, nein,* we could not take up guns against our own countrymen."

"They're our enemies if they don't share with us."

"Johann is right. We must show them we mean business."

"But someone might get killed. We want food, not war!"

The argument went on, and they could not agree. Papa was quiet, listening to both sides. At last he stood and held his hand up for attention.

"Wait, there is yet another way." The men fell silent and listened. "Bare hands are not enough, and guns are too much. But if each of us carried a club — a heavy stick in hand — they might be willing to listen to our demands."

There was a moment of silence.

"That's a good idea, Ernst, a sensible solution," said *Herr* Kaufmann.

"*Ja,* that's good."

So it was agreed the seven men would meet at dawn and go to New Braunfels in two wagons, clubs in hand, and bring back food for the colony.

Mina jumped down from the barrel as the men took their leave. She wanted to go with them in the morning, but she dared not ask. Girls and women had to wait at home for their men to return, and that bothered Mina. She wanted to be where things were happening, not waiting patiently at home. She was not patient. And she could not sit quietly.

When the men had left, Mina could hold it no longer. "Papa, can I go with you?"

Papa looked startled. *"Nein,* Mina. You know better than that. This is a job for men."

Mina stamped her foot angrily. "Why do men get to have all the excitement? I have spirit too, Papa."

"Mina! You must have more respect for your Papa," Lisette said.

Papa chuckled. "Don't worry, Lisette, Mina and I — we're like partners."

But Mina did not like being laughed at. All women could do to get respect was to have babies. It was better being a little girl — at least then she had not been expected to sit and wait.

"Please don't laugh at me, Papa." Mina turned, climbed up the ladder to the loft and threw herself down on her mattress. Her heart was pounding. It was not fair, not fair. She did not like being twelve years old and nearly a woman.

Darkness fell, and someone downstairs lighted a candle. Soft light came through the square opening in the loft floor.

Papa and Lisette talked quietly. It was a soothing sound. Mina was not mad at Papa or *Tante* Lisette — they were not to blame. That was the way the world was. Men have adventures and women have babies.

Mina turned over and lay on her back. The corn shucks in her mattress rustled. She felt very tired, and the voices from below were lulling her to sleep. Then she heard someone coming up the ladder. As she sat up she saw that it was Papa.

"I wanted to talk to you, Mina."

"Papa, I'm sorry I lost my temper."

"No, Mina, it's all right." Papa knelt down and took her hand in his rough ones. "I like your spirit. You have fire in your veins, and that's good. I don't want to put out

6

the fire. It's what makes you my special girl, my *kleine* Mina that I love so well. But . . ."

"I know, Papa, I can't go."

"If it were just you and me, Mina, you know I would take you along. But not with a group of men, all armed with clubs. Besides, *Tante* Lisette will need you."

Mina was too tired to argue.

Papa patted her hand in his. "Will you promise me something?"

"All right."

"Will you look after *Tante* Lisette? I'm worried about her in this heat, without proper food. Don't let her tire herself."

Women and babies, sit and wait. Mina looked at Papa in the dim light. His eyes searched her face with a worried look. She couldn't refuse him.

"All right, Papa, I promise." She threw her arms around him, and they held each other a moment.

"We've been through hard times together, Mina, and I know I can count on you." Papa got up, and went quietly downstairs. The light went out.

Hard times, Mina thought, and sighed deeply. She thought of Mama buried on that lonely windswept beach — lost to Texas. Mina's eyes filled with tears and overflowed. Tears ran down across her face and into her hair. She wiped them away roughly with her hands, turned over and closed her eyes.

The next she knew, men were talking outside the cabin, and the smell of acorn bread came up from below. Mina dressed hurriedly and climbed down the ladder.

Papa was already outside, and Lisette stood in the doorway watching. Every man had a club of some sort.

"We will return with food!" Papa exclaimed, raising his club on high.

"*Ja, ja,* with food!" the other men shouted.

Papa slapped one of the oxen on the rump, and off they started. The empty wagons rattled along. Papa

turned and waved. Mina and Lisette stood arm in arm in the doorway. Mina broke away and ran after the wagons, following them to the road.

"You take care, Papa," Mina waved again.

Papa turned back once more and looked at Mina with his sad eyes, smiled and nodded his head.

Mina stopped and watched the wagons and the group of men as the dust of their tracks rose up behind them. "Bring them back safely, please God," she said softly.

3

A SURPRISE

The bell in the *Vereinskirche* began to toll, but it was not Saturday. Mina was at the creek that ran behind the cabin, filling two buckets with water. She set them down, and hurried up to the cabin. Lisette was standing outside as the bell continued ringing.

"*Tante* Lisette, why is the church bell ringing?"

"I don't know . . . How strange it is." Lisette patted the perspiration from her forehead daintily with the corner of her apron.

"I'll run and see."

"All right, Mina. I'll come too." Lisette began untying her apron. "But you run ahead."

Mina was glad *Tante* Lisette did not ask her to wait. She ran barefoot down the sandy road toward the *Vereinskirche*, and turned on Market Street. There she could see the reason the bell was ringing.

Papa and the other men had returned, and the wagons were piled high with provisions. People were gath-

10

ering from all parts of the village. At first Mina could not find Papa.

"Your Papa is in the church ringing the bell," *Herr* Hessler told her.

Mina ran around the little octagonal church to the side where the door stood open. There was Papa in the middle of the room, pulling on the heavy rope that hung down from the bell in the tower. He was a short sturdy man. He is as strong as an ox, thought Mina as she watched him.

When he saw Mina, he let go of the rope and flung open his arms for her.

"Oh, Papa, you did it! You got food for us." They hugged each other close.

"*Ja*, now we will not go hungry for awhile. But how is *Tante* Lisette?"

"Fine, Papa. She's coming." Mina tossed her braids back, and looked at Papa. "Did you have to use the clubs?"

11

"Well, in a way we did." Papa chuckled. "The clubs helped them remember they had planned to send a share to us."

"I mean, did anyone have to fight?"

"*Nein*, Mina, if you carry a big club, you rarely have to use it. Just the threat is enough. But I have a surprise for you."

"What is it, Papa, tell me, tell me." Mina bounced on her toes.

"Wait until we are home, after supper." Papa started for the door. "Come along, now, let's find *Tante* Lisette, and get our share of the food. Tonight we shall have a feast"

A crowd had gathered around the two wagons, and the men began to hand out supplies.

"Two sacks of corn for each family," *Herr* Kaufmann said.

"Ernst!" Lisette ran to Papa, and they embraced. "Oh, Ernst, how glad I am you are home."

That evening they lingered at the table long after dark. It had been a satisfying supper — boiled potatoes cooked with salt pork, corn bread, and bacon.

Lisette lighted a candle and set it in the middle of the table. Mina could hardly wait to hear the surprise.

"Tell us now, Papa."

He leaned back in his chair, smiled at Mina, and began. "Well, the trip to New Braunfels served more than one purpose. I found out that the *Verein* has no more money — they are bankrupt."

"Oh, Ernst." Lisette covered her mouth with her hands.

"*Ja*, and they did not have good title to the land we were promised."

"Is *that* the surprise?" Mina asked in disbelief.

"You mean, Ernst, that we will never get the big tract of land the *Verein* promised?"

"*Nein, nein.*" Papa held up his hands as if to fend off

12

any more questions. "Just let me finish. The surprise is that the government of Texas has decided to give land grants to Germans. Six hundred and forty acre tracts on the other side of the Llano River. With that much land we can raise cattle. This country is too dry to survive on such a small piece of land as we have here. I understand that now. I will still have to haul supplies to earn money, but someday the land will be our living."

Papa stopped, and there was a moment of silence as Mina and Lisette waited for him to go on.

"What about Indians, Ernst? That is Comanche territory."

"*Ja*, but *Herr* Meusebach has made peace with them, and the land is open for settlement."

"I know that, Ernst." Lisette stood up from the table using her arms for support. "What I do not know is whether they can be trusted. And we would be miles from help — in the wilderness."

"Not completely alone, Lisette. I have talked with Emil and Heinrich, and they are both ready to move on to bigger tracts. We would make our own colony, and Mina would have her friend Anna nearby."

Lisette nodded her head thoughtfully.

"Think of the cholera, Lisette," Papa continued, "think how many families here have lost loved ones. We have been lucky so far, but how long will our luck hold out?"

Mina thought of the cart drawn by two black oxen that hauled the dead to the cemetery. She always turned away, for fear it could be a bad omen.

Lisette looked frightened then, and absently put her hand on her stomach as if to protect the baby from such evil. Papa changed to a happier subject.

"We three men would go ahead to build the cabins." He looked at Mina before she had time to object. "Mina will go to school until we are ready to move." He patted her arm. "After all, someone in this family must be able to speak English."

Mina knew there was no use arguing with Papa.

13

"Well, it's late, Ernst, and I'm tired." Lisette loosened the coiled braid at the back of her head, brought it over her shoulder, and proceeded to unbraid her hair. "Anyway, we can't decide such a matter tonight." She shook her long rippling hair back over her shoulder, and bent over to kiss Mina on the cheek and then Papa. "So, *gute Nacht.*"

"*Ja*, Lisette, I come directly."

When Mina and Papa were left alone at the table, he put his big hand on top of hers and looked at her closely. "So, what do you think, Mina? Are you willing to move on?"

"It sounds lonely, Papa. I . . . " She saw the eagerness in his eyes, the same look as when he wanted to come to Texas. It was a yearning, a restlessness that took hold of him. "Do you think it will be better than here?"

"I *know* it will, Mina." He squeezed her hand gently. "It is for this that we came to Texas. We did not come to starve on a few acres. We came to prosper, and in this country that means land and plenty of it."

Once Papa made up his mind to move on, there was no denying him. Mina felt herself being carried along by his enthusiasm.

He must have convinced Lisette too, because the next morning at breakfast she served them each a square of corn bread, sat down and announced, "Very well, Ernst, we will go. But it must be soon for I want to be settled when little Peter arrives." She leaned back and patted her stomach, and they all laughed together.

"*Jawohl*, Lisette, he shall be born in a fine cabin made snug against the cold of December. You will see." Papa jumped up, hugged Lisette and then Mina. "Then it's settled," he said, sitting back down and beginning to eat his corn bread rapidly.

"Ernst, you are not leaving today," Lisette said and smiled. "You have time to eat your breakfast."

But Papa's excitement had taken hold of him. He gulped down his coffee. "I must go and tell Heinrich and

14

Emil the good news so we can begin making preparations. There are only three months left."

Papa, *Herr* Kaufmann, *Herr* Hessler, and his son, Daniel, set off in August for the Llano River in Papa's wagon loaded with tools and supplies. Mina walked with them to the edge of the village in the cool of the early morning. There Papa put down his gun and hugged her.

"*Auf Wiedersehen,* Mina. Study your English so you can teach your Papa." He held her face in his hands a moment and kissed her forehead. "We'll be back before long."

"*Auf Wiedersehen* — Good-bye, Papa. Take care of yourself." Mina watched and waved as they bumped along the Indian trail, stirring up dust, and disappearing finally into the low rolling hills.

So, they were moving again. Mina thought back to their home in Wehrstedt with *Opa.* No one in the family had left the village for generations. *Opa's* house had been built by his father — a fine half-timbered house and barn — and Mina had known it as home for the first ten years of her life. But now . . . now she was a wanderer across the ocean and Texas.

4

OFF TO THE LLANO

Late in October the men returned. Papa looked tired, but his eyes were lively as he described the cabin. He sat forward, his elbows on his knees, cleaning his pipe at the hearth.

"The cabin is the best I have built," he said proudly. "It stands on a low bluff above Willow Creek. It even has a plank floor for the baby to crawl around on."

A floor! Mina had almost forgotten how it was to have a floor. *Opa's* house had a dark wooden floor, but since they had left Germany, the only floor she had known was the earth. She remembered how *Opa's* cat, Schnurri, used to lie in the square of sunlight that came through the casement window onto the polished floor.

"Oh, Papa, it sounds beautiful. A real floor again." Mina flipped her braid over her shoulder. "Do you think we could get a kitten? We could name it Schnurri."

Papa smiled sadly at Mina. "I had forgotten Schnurri. Of course we can."

16

A government scout and surveyor, William Allen, was in town, and he promised to accompany them from Fredericksburg to the Llano River. He said he had to pay a visit to the Comanche chief, Santana, and could offer them the added protection of his company.

Allen not only spoke the language of the Comanches, he spoke German as well as English. Papa asked him to speak in English so that they could learn the language of their "new" fatherland.

It was early in the morning when the three families started out in their wagons pulled by ox teams. The wagons creaked under heavy loads, and the yoke chains rattled with every step. Tied to the side of the Jordans' wagon was a plow and hoe, and hanging from a rope, a sealed pail of milk swayed to and fro. By afternoon it would be churned into butter. Liesel, their spotted milch cow, was tied to the back.

Mina skipped along beside the wagon feeling excitement at the thought of heading for a new home. *Tante* Lisette walked beside Papa. The baby would arrive in a few weeks, and she could not take the jolting of the wagon.

The Jordans' wagon was first in line behind William Allen on Yack, a bay horse that had a white blaze down its forehead and two white feet. Mina longed to ride that beautiful prancing horse. Maybe tomorrow she would ask Mister Allen. The Kaufmanns were second in line, then the Hesslers, followed by the small herd of longhorn cattle.

Mina stopped and turned to wait for the Kaufmann family's wagon to come alongside. Anna walked beside her father and mother obediently. She had her father's fine features and dark hair which was neatly braided, every strand in place. She never seemed to get mussed or dirty.

"Let's sing something, Anna."

"All right, how about *Over on the Green Meadow*."

So they sang as they walked hand in hand, swinging

17

their arms gaily. Mina looked back beyond the Hesslers' wagon and saw Daniel, his blond shock of hair shining in the sun. He was riding his horse with his little brother behind. It was his job to keep the cattle following the wagons. Daniel looked very grownup. Well, thought Mina, he *is* fifteen, and that is practically a man.

"You know, Anna," Mina squeezed her hand a little, "I think Daniel Hessler is very handsome."

"So do I."

"Maybe I'll ask him to marry me someday!" The two girls were convulsed with giggles.

When Anna caught her breath she said, "Mina, you say the craziest things!"

"I know, that's because I *am* crazy." Mina stuck her tongue out one side of her mouth and crossed her eyes. Again the girls went into gales of giggles. Mina looked back at Daniel, but he didn't seem to notice them.

"Get along," Daniel shouted at one cow that began to stray. He rode around to the other side to head her back to the herd. "Hey! Get along now."

The day wore on, and the girls were quieter. Dust swirled up from beneath the animals' hoofs. Mina could feel it clogging her throat and coating her face. By late afternoon they came to a sandy creek crossing and stopped to camp. The wagons pulled alongside the clear meandering creek, and the men began to unhitch the oxen. Mina ran to Liesel, untied her from the wagon, and took her to the water. She stroked the smooth spotted neck as Liesel drank.

William Allen rode a short way up the creek. Suddenly, his horse whinnied and tossed its head about as if to loosen the reins. Allen looked up the creek. "Easy Yack, take it easy." He patted the horse's neck and rode back to the campsite.

"Don't be alarmed. There's an Indian camp a few yards upstream, but I think they're Lipans. Just stay here while I go and talk to them."

Could they be from Custaleta's camp, Mina wondered?

"Can I go with you, Mister Allen?"

William Allen looked at her in a quizzical way for a moment. Even though he was young his eyes were serious and deep-set in his thin face. "Why sure, *Fräulein*. Climb up here behind me." Then looking at Papa, "Do you mind, Ernst? She would show them we are peaceful."

Papa looked at Mina. "Very well, William, I trust you and your way with Indians. Besides Mina has her own way with them too."

Papa made a stirrup with his hands, and Mina put one foot there as Mister Allen offered her his hand. She flung her other leg over the horse's back, and was suddenly astride Yack behind the saddle. The horse gave a little start.

"Mina, that's not the way a lady rides," Papa said, looking half amused. "A lady rides sidesaddle."

"But Papa, this is the way Amaya rides." She tightened her legs against Yack's broad sides. Besides, I would slide right off."

"What would your mother say if she saw you?"

That sobered Mina for a moment. "I know, Papa. She would say,'Mina, you must act more like a lady.'"

"*Ja*, she would say that," Papa agreed, nodding his head.

"But I doubt she would want me to fall off!" Mina brightened that she had thought of such a good argument.

"Perhaps you are right," Papa chuckled and waved them off.

Mina felt Yack's strength beneath her as he lurched forward. She held on to the back of the saddle with both hands. Her right hand was almost touching the polished wooden handle of Mister Allen's Colt revolver in its holster.

"Can you really shoot five times without reloading?"

"Yep." Mister Allen patted the holster. "It sure is a friend in need."

5

SOME ADVICE

As they came close to the Indian camp William Allen slowed Yack to a walk, shouted a greeting, and made a signal of peace by raising his right arm bent at the elbow.

The four Indian men who watched their approach returned the signal. Allen reined in Yack, got off, and tied him to a branch.

"You wait, Mina, I'll just have a word with them." He took a small bag out of his buckskin shirt pocket. "Glass beads. I'm going to do a little trading."

Mina watched as they talked. Yack tossed his mane, and turned to look at the strange rider on his back. One of the men called something to an Indian squaw, and she brought a leg of meat and gave it to Allen. In exchange he gave them the bag of beads. There were more words Mina could not understand. Then the scout returned to Mina and Yack.

"Well, Mina, here's a leg of bear for our supper. A quick hunt, eh?"

"Jawohl."

"Say, *Fräulein*, why don't you sit in the saddle. I'll crawl up behind and handle this bear, and you see if you can handle Yack."

Mina had watched Mister Allen closely, and thought she could do it.

He handed her the reins. "Now just hold him back till I get on."

Yack took a few steps backward as Allen mounted. Then they waved to the Indians.

"It's just as I thought, Mina. They're Lipans. Indians, on their way to Fredericksburg to trade — Custaleta's people. They're camping near the Llano River now — not too far from your place.

Mina's heart leaped. She had thought she would never see Chief Custaleta or Amaya again. It was a good feeling to know that friendly Indians would be nearby.

"All right, *Fräulein*, are you ready?"

"*Ja.*"

"Then loosen up on the reins and give him a nudge with your heels."

Yack started off and went quickly into a trot. He was a young and responsive animal, full of energy.

Back at the wagons a fire was blazing.

"Now, pull back on the reins."

"Ho there, Yack," Mina commanded in as deep a voice as she could manage.

William Allen dismounted. "Look what we have here." He held the bear leg over his head like a victorious warrior.

They made a spit of branches and soon had the meat roasting and dripping into the fire.

The stars came out, and still they sat around the campfire talking.

"No, you don't have to worry about the Lipans along the Llano, Ernst," Allen was saying. "But I'd be a little wary of the Comanches. I don't trust them myself — even though John Meusebach made a treaty with Chief Buffalo Hump. Their warriors roam in small bands and do as they please."

Mister Allen took his Colt revolver out of the holster and examined it. The barrel gleamed in the firelight.

"Fact of the matter is," he continued, "the Lipans hate the Comanches more than they ever hated any white man. They've been enemies for years. When I was riding with the Texas Rangers a while back, we had a Lipan-Apache scout. He led us to many a Comanche camp, and we attacked with these little fire-spitters." He held up his five-shot revolver.

Daniel watched Mister Allen's every move and listened intently as he talked. Maybe he wished to be like William Allen. Daniel was already the best marksman of all the men, the best hunter too.

"I'm not trying to scare you folk," Allen continued, "but you would do well to make an alliance with Custaleta. Meanwhile, you should decide on some kind of signal for help — like two shots fired in rapid succession — in case of Comanche attack on one of your cabins."

"*Attack!*" Lisette paled. "Are we likely to be attacked, Mister Allen?"

"No, not likely. It's just a precaution. I didn't mean to alarm you, *Frau* Jordan."

"Well," Papa said as he stood up, "we should get some sleep now so we can start early."

Mina got her blanket and pillow from the wagon and, with Anna, found a place near the fire where the grass was thick. They spread out their blankets and lay down. Mina pulled hers close around her, for the air had a chill. The pulsing song of the crickets made a soothing lullaby.

"Mina?" Anna said turning over toward her.

"Hmmh?"

"Are you scared?"

"Of what?"

"Comanches."

"Not with Mister Allen here," Mina said.

"Remember the night the panther woke us up and jumped out of the tree right in front of us?"

A shudder passed through Mina as she remembered. "What if one came tonight, Anna? And pounced right in the middle of your stomach?" With that, Mina lunged at Anna's dark form with her hands.

Anna screamed.

"Girls, girls, quiet now," Papa said from the wagon where he slept beside Lisette.

"Anna, go to sleep, you and Mina," *Herr* Kaufmann said.

"Shhhh," Mina and Anna said to each other and giggled. Mina clamped her hand over her mouth to keep from exploding with laughter. She saw Daniel on the other side of the fire as he lay back down to sleep.

Occasionally a giggle would escape from Mina or Anna, but at last Mina began to feel drowsy.

Once again they were camped out in the wilderness, and that old feeling crept back. It was that lonely feeling that came in the dark when it seemed as if there were no other people in the whole world. Of course, Mina knew there were lots of other people out there — even Comanches. Her eyes popped open. But soon, even thoughts of Comanches could not keep her eyelids from closing and she sank into sleep.

6

THE PROMISED LAND

They crossed the wide Llano River at a shallow place. The water was clear, and ran rapidly over slabs of rock.

William Allen called a halt in midstream, and the oxen and cattle were allowed to drink their fill. He pointed downstream. "Chief Custaleta's camp is about two miles down that way."

Mina looked in that direction but could see nothing. She scooped some water and drank from her cupped hands. The hem of her skirt got soaking wet, but she didn't mind. Suddenly Daniel splashed water on her, and ran with long strides toward the opposite bank.

Mina screamed, "I'll get you, Daniel Hessler," and ran after him, holding her skirt above the water. Before she could catch up he reached the other side, turned, and faced her, laughing. His blond hair slanted across his forehead, and he tossed it back with a shake of his head.

Seeing him laugh made Mina angry, and she rushed

up and began pummeling him with her fists. He put up his arms for protection.

"Oh, please stop, Mina," he pled mockingly. Then he grabbed her arms, and no matter how she struggled she could not hit him. He was very strong.

"Oh, I hate you, Daniel Hessler!"

Daniel let go and ran off, laughing. Mina chased him around the wagons, but he was too fast for her and she gave up at last. She was out of breath and her heart was beating rapidly. She joined Papa beside their wagon as they walked on. Daniel went back to herding the cattle.

"Mina, remember what your Mama always said. You must act like a lady," Papa said.

"Very well, Papa, but nobody told Daniel to act like a gentleman." Mina flipped her braids over her shoulders defiantly.

Papa threw back his head and laughed. In spite of herself Mina smiled. Maybe Daniel did like her after all.

When they came to a fork in the trail, William Allen had to leave them. He was taking the left toward Santana's camp, and they were veering right toward their promised land.

"Well, I'll say farewell here." Allen got off Yack and shook hands with all of the men including Daniel. He walked to Mina and took out a little leather bag which he handed to her. "I like your spirit, *Fräulein*. You're a girl, but you think like a man!"

Mina shrugged. "I think like I think," she declared, "and not like I'm supposed to. Sometimes, it gets me into trouble."

Papa and Mister Allen laughed.

"And someday, it may get you *out* of trouble, *Fräulein*," Mister Allen said.

Mina smiled at him. She pulled open the drawstring bag and peeked inside. It was filled with glass beads of every color and there was a small mirror.

25

"Just a little something to trade with the Indians," Allen said as he mounted Yack.

"Why that's very thoughtful of you, Mister Allen."

As he started off, he turned in his saddle and called back, "I'll try to stop by for a visit on my next trip. Good luck to you."

"*Ja*, do that," Lisette called.

"Good luck, Mister Allen." Mina waved. She hated to see him go. She would miss him and his prancing horse and his stories. They all watched until he disappeared in the brush.

"Well, we must move along." Papa pulled out a surveyor's map. "We only have a short distance to go. Just across this small creek to that big live oak and we are there." He pointed to the spot on the map.

Papa shouldered his gun, whistled at the oxen, and the wagon wheels began to turn again. The trail had given out, and they were traveling along a small creek.

At a place where the creek turned sharply, the small group crossed over. Mina looked upstream and saw a deer, startled while drinking, that darted into the bushes.

"Papa, did you see it? A deer?"

"Where?"

"Just up there."

It was already gone, quickly and silently.

"Looks like Daniel will have good hunting. Even I should have no trouble bringing in meat."

At the top of a rise they could see across a broad valley.

"There's Willow Creek!" Papa shouted.

Soon they came to the giant live oak. Papa signaled a stop.

"What is it, Ernst? Why do we stop here?" Lisette asked.

"Because, now we are on our land." He motioned them to gather around. "This grass, that tree, as far as your eyes can see — this is our promised land."

Papa's excitement stirred Mina. She loved to see him

26

so full of life and expectation. He had not been that way back in Germany, not until they had decided to come to Texas. In spite of all that had happened to them Papa was a new man.

The other wagons had come alongside, and everyone gathered around.

"Let us pray and give thanks to God," Papa said. They stood in a half circle and bowed their heads.

Father, we thank Thee
For this fair land,
And for our safe journey.
Bless our labors here;
May our German seed
Thrive in this Texas soil. Amen.

"Amen," the group responded.

7

A RATTLE IN THE GRASS

A little further on they came in sight of the Jordans' log cabin overlooking the creek. Mina could not wait for the slow plodding oxen.

"Anna, come on!" Together, hand in hand, the girls ran along the creek, up the rise and stopped. The side of the cabin faced the creek, and a friendly covered porch on the front sheltered the door. Most wonderful of all was a high loft window in the gable facing the creek. That would be Mina's window. From there she could open the shutter and look across to Anna's cabin on the other side, perhaps even farther.

The grass was tall and the girls waded through it toward the cabin. Suddenly, directly in front of them there was a raspy rattling. Mina looked down. There, no more than three feet before them, lay a coiled rattlesnake. Its forked tongue flicked in and out, and the tip of its tail was turned up, rattling. Mina squeezed Anna's hand.

Snake! Anna screamed, but neither of them moved.

Mina was transfixed by the creature. "Don't move, Anna. Keep still or it will strike."

Anna held her breath, and the girls looked at the snake as the snake looked at the girls. Mina could hear excited voices at the wagons and then someone walking slowly, brushing carefully through the tall grass. The snake vibrated its rattles even more violently.

"Don't move," came a whispered command from Daniel.

Mina didn't take her eyes off the rattlesnake. She was ready to leap should he strike. Daniel edged up beside her, his shotgun leveled at the snake. He stopped, took aim, and fired. The blast was deafening. Mina's hands flew to her ears.

The snake's head was blown off and its body uncoiled and writhed about.

Anna turned and ran screaming and crying as the grownups rushed toward them. Before they all arrived Mina looked at Daniel standing beside her. His eyes were on the snake's body.

"You're a good shot," Mina's voice was barely audible, but Daniel heard. He looked at her and smiled.

Papa and the men rushed up, and *Herr* Kaufmann had a hoe, ready to kill the snake if Daniel had missed. The women were close behind. They all watched the snake as its writhing diminished, and it lay still with only an occasional jerk.

Then Papa spoke. "Let this be a warning to all of us. There are dangers here on the frontier. We must be alert for them, always alert."

"Well, at least we don't have cholera to worry about, like in town," *Frau* Kaufmann said, a look of relief on her broad peasant face.

"No, only rattlesnakes and Comanches!" Lisette said.

Everyone laughed, including Mina. At the same time, she felt a vague dread about Comanches. Snakes she could watch out for, but Comanches . . .

Papa dug a hole and buried the snake's head. *Herr* Hessler took the body, laid it out on a flat rock, and slit the skin from top to bottom.

"It will make a fine belt," he said.

Daniel and Mina peeled the skin off. Anna would only look between her fingers, and then cover her face again.

"Oh, Mina, how can you do that?"

It was not a pleasant task, yet Mina felt she had to know about everything, and not hide from it. Inside the naked body, she could see that the snake's heart continued to pulse. It was as if the snake were still alive.

"Poor snake," Mina said aloud.

"I'm glad it's *poor snake* instead of *poor Mina and Anna!*" Lisette hugged her around the shoulders.

"*Jawohl,*" Papa said.

"Well, folks, it's time we move on to our cabin," said *Herr* Kaufmann.

Daniel picked up the snake. "Anyone for rattlesnake meat?"

"Ugh," Anna clutched her throat and screwed up her usually placid face.

After the Hesslers and Kaufmanns had driven on across Willow Creek, Papa, Mina, and Lisette stood before their cabin.

"So, how do you like it?"

Lisette nodded her head and smiled. Papa put his arm around her, and she rested her head against his shoulder. He put his other arm around Mina.

"Papa, did you make that window in the loft for me?"

"That I did, Mina."

She tightened her arm around his waist. "It *is* the best cabin."

"So, let's unload this wagon," Papa said.

"First the clock, Papa. The clock has to be wound and put in place over the mantel before we can start living here." Mina climbed into the wagon and began to look

31

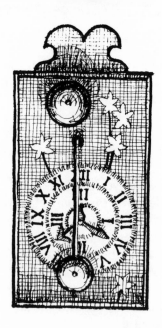

about. "*Tante* Lisette, do you remember where we packed it?"

"*Ja*, Mina, in the clothing box just behind the seat."

Mina lifted the latch of the box, looked beneath some clothes, and there it was — the little Black Forest wall clock *Opa* had given them when they left Germany. White *Edelweiss* flowers were painted around its face. Mina picked it up tenderly, and with Papa and Lisette, stepped onto the porch and entered the cabin.

It was bigger than their first cabin. There were two rooms downstairs and a ladder leading up to Mina's loft. The floor beneath her feet was solid and smooth.

"Oh, Ernst, it's no wonder you were so tired when you returned," Lisette said and put her hands to her cheeks in amazement.

"And look," Papa walked to the fireplace and pointed above the mantel. "Look, here is the peg for hanging the clock."

Mina hung it and started the small brass pendulum. *Ticktock, ticktock.*

"Now," Mina said, her hands on her hips, "our new life has begun."

32

8

TANTE LISETTE'S TIME

One night in November a strange moan awakened Mina. She sat up and listened. Nothing. What was it? Her heart pounded hard against her chest. Alone in the loft she sat waiting for the sound to come again. Darkness pushed in on her, and she dared not get out of bed. She shivered and pulled the blankets around her shoulders.

Then it came again — from downstairs. Someone lighted a candle.

"What is it, Papa?" Mina leaned over to look into the room below.

Papa came out of the adjoining room putting on his shirt hurriedly and looked up at her.

"*Tante* Lisette — her time has come. I'm going for *Frau* Kaufmann. You come down and stay with her, Mina," Papa turned as he went out the door, "and build up a fire." Papa's eyes were intense, but he managed a brief smile at her and was gone.

Mina pulled on her house slippers and wrapper, for it

had grown cold in the cabin. She hurried down the ladder, bolted the door, and went into Lisette's room.

A candle beside the bed lit Lisette's delicate features. Her eyes were closed, and her mouth was slightly open. Although the room was cold, her forehead was damp with perspiration, and strands of dark hair stuck to her cheeks. Mina stood at the door a moment, not knowing what to do. Then Lisette's pale face was suddenly contorted, her body grew rigid, and another moan filled the room.

Mina rushed to her bed. "*Tante* Lisette." She smoothed back the strands of hair. What if the baby should come before Papa returned?

Then Lisette relaxed and her body went limp again. She opened her eyes, looked at Mina, and smiled faintly.

"It's all right, Mina. Don't worry."

But Lisette did not look all right, and she was breathing heavily. Sometimes women died in childbirth. That thought sent a pang of fear through Mina, and she took Lisette's hand in hers.

Mina's thoughts flew back to that terrible night on the beach when Mama died, left her and Papa. She had just stopped breathing, and they had to put her in a box and under the ground. Mina shuddered when she thought of covering Mama's casket with dirt. It didn't seem right. How could her spirit escape and go to heaven? She wondered if Mama was in heaven now looking down on her.

Mina shivered in the cold room. "I'll go and build up the fire."

Lisette's eyes were closed again, but she nodded to Mina.

The only sound was the *ticktock* of the clock. It was usually a comforting sound, but tonight it seemed lonely and hollow. She must get a fire going.

Papa had banked the coals, so Mina gently raked the ashes away. With a hatchet she splintered some thin pieces of wood from a split log, and lay them lightly on

34

the glowing coals, crossing this way and that. They began to smoke, and suddenly burst into flame. Mina liked the tiny flame. It had life and was a good omen of life springing up. She fed the fire carefully with larger and larger pieces. Never in her life had she wanted to keep a flame going as much an now. The fire popped sharply and began to envelop the larger logs she placed on it.

"*Ohhhhhhh,*" Lisette began to moan again, and Mina ran back to the bed and took her hand. Lisette squeezed so hard Mina thought her knuckles would break.

After Lisette relaxed her tight grip, Mina stroked her forehead again.

"Papa and *Frau* Kaufmann will be here soon," she tried to sound cheery.

"When, Mina?" Lisette's voice was soft.

"Any minute now," she lied. Mina knew that it would take time for Papa to cross the creek in the dark and find his way to the Kaufmanns' cabin. Then, *Frau* Kaufmann would have to dress, and that took time. What if they did not make it before the baby came? What if she was the only one to help *Tante* Lisette? Mina's heart renewed its rapid pounding.

"I'll get a damp cloth and be right back."

Mina poured a bucket of water into the black pot and hung it over the fire. Then she dampened a cloth, hurried back to Lisette, and gently wiped her face. Lisette smiled at her.

"You're a good girl, Mina."

As the minutes went by, Mina sat by Lisette, holding her hand, hoping and praying for Papa to come. Once, between Lisette's labor pains, Mina was so weary that she began to doze, and was startled at the painful squeezing of her hand.

9

PETER

Mina heard voices outside — it was Papa. She ran and unbolted the door.

Frau Kaufmann bustled right in, moving quickly to remove her cape and bonnet and hang them on a peg by the door. Papa rushed in to Lisette.

Frau Kaufmann looked at Mina, took her hand and patted it. "Stop worrying, child, I have helped birth many a baby. Now, bring me some hot water and towels."

Mina did as she was told, and *Frau* Kaufmann went in to Lisette.

"I'm here now, Lisette. All is well."

Lisette heaved a deep sigh of relief. "Thank you, Eva. How much longer will it be?"

"Not long. Now, Ernst, you go in the other room."

Mina brought the towels, and a pot of steaming water, and set them on the chest beside the bed. She returned to sit beside the fire with Papa, to wait or fetch whatever was needed. *Frau* Kaufmann closed the door.

Lisette's groans and cries became more frequent.

Each time, Papa jumped up and paced about the room nervously. The clock ticked away the minutes and hours of the night. The fire popped and gave out a warm glow. Mina dozed off once in the rocking chair. She seemed to be struggling to push open a door that pushed back at her. She had to open it. Someone was calling her from the other side.

Suddenly a scream pierced Mina's slumber — an agonized scream. Mina opened her eyes, remembering where she was and what was happening. Papa was standing stock-still, waiting. Mina ran to him.

"Oh, Papa, I'll never get married and have a baby."

Papa wrapped Mina in his arms. "Now, now, Mina, don't say that."

"But I mean it, Papa."

Then a miracle happened. There was a tiny hollow cry.

Mina and Papa looked at each other in wonder. There were no more sounds from Lisette, only the baby's continuing cry.

In a while *Frau* Kaufmann opened the door and came toward them smiling, with a tiny bundle held in her arms.

"Ernst, you have a son!" She looked toward Mina, "a baby brother."

Papa whooped for joy, and took the bundle carefully from *Frau* Kaufmann. Mina stood on her tiptoes to look at him.

"*Ja*, it's Peter all right."

Papa chuckled and handed him to Mina. "Would you like to hold him?"

Mina took Peter gently. He was so light and peaceful, sound asleep. He made some smacking sounds with his tiny new mouth.

Together they went in to Lisette. There she lay, propped up on pillows, smiling and peaceful. Papa went over and kissed her forehead. Was this the same Lisette, Mina wondered. So calm and beautiful? The pain in her eyes had vanished, and so, it seemed, had the memory of it. Her face was as radiant as that day she had said "Oh, yes" to Papa's blurted proposal of marriage. Mina thought of a painting of the Virgin Mary holding baby Jesus that hung in the church in Wehrstedt. The face in the painting had glowed with a special light as Mary looked down at the baby in her arms. *Tante* Lisette's face was the same.

In the days that followed, baby Peter demanded a lot of attention from Lisette and Papa. They did not have as much time for Mina.

Sometimes she even wished Peter had never been born. She knew it was wrong to have such feelings, but for so long she had been Papa's only one, his *kleine* Mina. Now she had to share him.

One evening Papa sat rocking Peter to sleep cradled against his coarse linsey shirt, humming a lullaby. His sad eyes seemed to be looking back to another time, another place.

"Did you rock me like that when I was a baby?" Mina asked as she set the table for supper. She hadn't meant to let her thoughts come out, but now the words hung in the stillness of the cabin. Only the ticking clock and sizzling fire kept going.

Papa looked at her for a moment. Then without saying a word, he got up and gently put Peter down in his cradle. He came to Mina and wrapped his arms around her as she held the utensils in one hand.

"I should say I did, my *kleine* Mina, I should say I did." He chuckled, "Only, you never seemed to want to give up and close your eyes — always waving your little arms, trying to touch my beard." He gave her a squeeze. "No one will ever take your place in my heart, Mina, you know that."

Mina felt tears gather in her eyes, and as Papa loosened his arms and looked into her face, she dropped a fork onto the floor.

"Ah, visitors coming!" Lisette said. "It's a sure sign when a fork falls."

Mina felt happiness welling up inside her. Things were changing, but some things never changed. She understood that now.

Besides, visitors were coming — perhaps for Christmas.

10

CHRISTMAS COMES AGAIN

Mina looked out the loft window. Papa had made a table attached to the wall under the window, and there Mina placed her quill pen, bottle of ink, and writing paper she had brought from Germany. From her chair she could look out over Willow Creek where the tall pecan trees and willows along its banks were bare of leaves. On the other side stood Anna's cabin with smoke rising from the chimney.

Downstairs the cabin door was open. It was a warm day for December, and Mina stepped out into the morning sunlight.

She could hear the dull thud of Papa's axe hitting a log as he chopped wood behind the cabin. Mina picked up a bucket and started toward the rain barrel that stood at the end of the porch.

Suddenly she heard hoofbeats on the road down along the creek.

"Papa, someone is coming!"

Papa came to the porch still holding the axe, and

they both looked in the direction of the sound. Lisette stood in the doorway cradling Peter in her arms.

A man on horseback rode into sight leading another horse. "Hello," he called, and raising one arm slightly, he waved to them. *"Wie geht's?"*

Mina recoqnized his voice and his broad shouldered slouch in the saddle.

"Why, it's Mister Allen!" Mina ran down to meet him, her braids flying.

Yack was prancing proudly with his head held high. William Allen's thin face broke into a smile as Mina reached him and walked beside Yack to the cabin.

"Hello, Mister Allen. What a surprise." Then she remembered the fork. *"Of course! You're the visitor."*

William Allen looked at her in a quizzical way, not understanding.

"You see, I dropped a fork, so we knew someone was coming." Mina put her hands on her hips and looked back at the small black horse Allen was leading.

The horse shook his head to be rid of the reins tied to Yack's saddle, and looked curiously at Mina with his alert black eyes. He had one white forefoot.

"Where did you get another horse?"

"Oh, I did some Indian trading. See his slit ears — he's a Comanche horse." They stopped, Allen dismounted and untied the reins. "Do you like him?"

"He's beautiful," Mina said moving closer. "Where are you taking him?"

Allen smiled. "Well, I'm taking him to a young friend of mine for a Christmas present."

Mina looked into William Allen's face closely. Her heart began to pound. She saw merriment in his pale blue eyes. What did he mean, she wondered? Could he be talking about me — a horse for me? Mina caught her breath.

"Do you mean me?" Her question hung in the air for a moment.

41

Then Allen laughed. He seemed to be enjoying her bewilderment.

"A horse for me?" Mina repeated in disbelief.

"Yep."

Mina began to jump around in circles clapping her hands. William Allen had to hold the reins as the little black horse began to back away from such frightening activity.

"Papa, Mister Allen has brought me a horse for Christmas."

Papa was standing just behind Mina, watching and listening. He shook hands with Allen and exchanged greetings.

"We can never repay you for such a gift, William."

"No need to, Ernst. Mina has already done that."

Papa chuckled. "Well, you have to stay for Christmas anyway."

"Thanks, don't mind if I do. I'm a bit weary of the trail." The scout took off his hat to greet Lisette and baby Peter.

"We're delighted to have you stay with us, William," Lisette said.

Company for Christmas! Mina liked that. Her friend knew so many stories and he had done so many exciting things.

"What is the horse's name?" Mina asked.

"The Comanches called him Tucan, which means night."

Mina went slowly over to the horse, put out her hand to pet his forehead. Tucan jerked his head up and away, but Mina tried again. "Tucan," she said softly. This time he let her touch him, and the horse's shoulder quivered slightly. Tucan seemed a magical name, as though he came from a dream world. His long silky mane was black as night.

"Want to ride him?" Mister Allen asked.

"Sure." Mina flipped her braids back over her shoulders.

42

Papa made a stirrup with his hands. Tucan turned his head to look as Mina started to get on.

"Easy now, Tucan," Allen said, "this young lady is your new mistress. You're going to like her better than that Comanche warrior."

"Tucan," Mina said softly and stroked his neck. She put her other hand on his bare back and pulled herself up. He backed up a little until the slack in the reins was taken up. Mina held on to his mane with both hands.

"Easy, Tucan, easy." William Allen came close to him and put his hand on Tucan's neck. "Soon as he is used to you, he'll let you get on without any trouble. Just talk to him, Mina."

Allen led Tucan around with Mina on his back. Mina leaned forward, resting her head on his neck and talked to him.

"You'll like me, Tucan, I know you will."

Tucan turned his ears around toward Mina.

"We'll be the best of friends." She stroked his silky mane.

Mina felt as one with Tucan as her body rocked in motion with his swaying gait. She thought of herself flying across the countryside on his back. She could even go to visit Amaya at the Indian camp. How proud she would be to ride up on a horse like Tucan.

After awhile Allen handed her the reins, and she rode Tucan around and around the cabin. Several times he turned his head to look at her.

Papa and Mister Allen watched as she rode by.

"Doing just fine, young lady. In a few days Tucan will be yours," Mister Allen called.

William Allen stayed for Christmas. Daniel had shot a deer, and they cooked it over an open fire near the live oak in front of the Jordans' cabin.

On Christmas Eve the Kaufmanns and Hesslers came. They all sat around the heavy plank table on

43

benches and ate venison, corn bread with butter, and sweet potatoes, while Peter slept in his cradle.

The *Weihnachtsbaum*, a cedar tree, glowed with its candlelight blossoms in the corner of the room. The branches were hung with honey cookies Lisette and Mina had made the day before.

Afterward they all sang as Papa played on his harmonica:

Der Christbaum ist der schönste Baum,
Den wir auf Erden kennen.

Mina looked at Daniel across the table. She did not understand the stirring inside her whenever he was around.

Daniel paid her little attention when Mister Allen began to tell stories. Somehow Daniel's aloofness made her like him all the more, though at the same time she hated him for it.

She liked him because already he was so manly, but she did not like the way he ignored her. Too, it bothered her that Daniel, being a boy, could have adventures like Mister Allen, while she could not have such adventures. Or could she? She had a horse now.

Mina imagined herself as an Indian agent, dressed in deerskin, riding away on Tucan. She would look back at Daniel standing beside the cabin and call, *I'll be back in two or three weeks. Take care of everything while I'm gone.* Then she would gallop away with Tucan's long black mane flying. Mina giggled at her thoughts.

Late that night she lay awake in the loft. It had been their best Christmastime in Texas. Much different from that first Christmas on the beach where they landed. Then she had been homesick for Germany, and they had no roof over their heads and little to eat. Yet somehow Christmas had come upon them, and their spirits rose to meet it. Mina thought of how she and Anna had searched for something to be a *Tannenbaum*, and found a piece of driftwood — a pitiful old branch — which they planted in the sand. Everyone had hung something on the bare limbs. Tears came to her eyes now as she remembered lighting the candles and standing around the tree singing *O Tannenbaum.* Christmas had arrived, in spite of the misery all around. That was what had made it so sweet, although she had not known it at the time.

Her thoughts were interrupted by someone coming up the ladder.

"Papa?"

"*Ja,* Mina."

He set a candle on the table and pulled the chair up beside her bed.

"Mina, I must leave for San Antonio tomorrow to do a hauling job that Mister Allen has told me about. We need the money and we need supplies."

"Can I . . ." Mina stopped. She saw by the look in Papa's eyes that she could not.

"*Nein,* Mina, you need to be here. You are the only one who knows how to fire the shotgun, and I will leave it for you." He studied her face closely for a reply.

Mina nodded her head. "All right, Papa."

"And remember, if there is any trouble, fire two shots to call *Herr* Kaufmann and the Hesslers."

"*Ja,* I know, Papa."

"Goodnight then." He patted her arm and went down the ladder.

11

HONEY COOKIES AND A SONG

While Papa was away Mina did not like falling to sleep at night. She could never quite relax and give herself up to the enveloping darkness. Only *Tante* Lisette and Peter were downstairs.

Any strange sound from outside the cabin set Mina on edge, and her body became tense and rigid as she listened. Usually there was some explanation — Tucan stepping on a twig, or an armadillo burrowing in his hole. It was hard to fall asleep when she was alert to every sound. Sleep only came when she was so tired Indians could have carried her away without even a cry.

In the morning when she awakened she would whisper a prayer, "Thank you, God, for bringing us safely through the night." Scary thoughts fled before the light of day, and Mina went about her chores.

Papa had left a big stack of chopped wood by the washing tree back of the cabin. "Remember, Mina, work makes life sweet," he said. So every morning Mina carried in enough logs to last for the day, and put them beside the fireplace. She milked Liesel, tidied the house, swept the floor, and carried in the water.

Mina supposed that Papa meant work *completed* made life sweet. It was true, she thought as she contemplated the clean house with wood stacked by the fire.

In the evenings when Peter slept soundly in his cradle, Lisette would sometimes give Mina lessons in penmanship or listen as she read aloud from Murray's *English Reader*.

One Saturday after the noon meal, Lisette put Peter in his cradle, and sat down to churn, rocking the cradle with her foot and singing a little mother-song to him. Papa had been away for three weeks, and it seemed very lonely in the cabin.

"*Tante* Lisette, my chores are finished. May I go to Anna's on Tucan?" She really wanted to go to the Hesslers' too, but did not say so.

"All right, Mina. I need you to take some cookies to Anna and *Frau* Hessler also." There was a twinkle in her eyes, and Mina felt embarrased that Lisette seemed to have read her mind.

Mina took the honey cookies and skipped out the open door. Tucan was grazing in the field beyond the garden. She got the bridle from a peg on the front porch and called to him. The little horse stopped grazing, lifted his head, and looked at her. His front legs were hobbled. She walked out to meet him.

"Come, Tucan. How would you like me to unhobble you so you can stretch out your legs?" She stroked his neck and let him eat a cookie from her hand. His warm moist lips scoured her palm for crumbs. She gave him another.

Mina had ridden Tucan every day she could. He always came when she called, and seemed to enjoy the rides together as much as she did. Mina liked to ride fast, galloping along the road by the creek. She clung to him with her legs and felt her loose hair lifted by the wind.

"You ride like a wild Indian," Lisette had said more

than once. "If it weren't for your blonde hair, I couldn't tell the difference."

Now, she untied the hobble, and carefully put on the bridle. Holding onto his withers, Mina gave a jump and was on his back.

At the creek, Tucan pulled on the reins, and she let him drink his fill. Then they splashed through and up the bank to the Kaufmanns' cabin. Anna was helping her mother wash by stirring the clothes with a stick in the big black kettle that hung over the fire.

"Hello," Mina called as she approached the cabin.

Anna looked up from her stirring as Mina dismounted. "Where are you going?"

"*Tante* Lisette made some honey cookies for you and the Hesslers." Mina tied Tucan to a tree. I'm delivering them. Want to go with me?"

"I have to ask Mama." Anna took the cookies to her mother who was rinsing the clothes in another pot. "Look what Mina brought!"

"Why, how nice." *Frau* Kaufmann smoothed back a strand of hair with her arm. "Thank you, Mina."

"May I go with Mina to deliver cookies to the Hesslers?"

Frau Kaufmann looked at them both for a moment in her tired way. "Very well, girls, if you'll help wring these clothes and hang them on the fence first."

Frau Kaufmann lifted each article out of the kettle with the stick and onto a flat rock. There they steamed in the cold air and dripped until cool enough to handle. Anna and Mina each took one end and twisted until all the water had been wrung out, and draped each piece over the fence to dry in the sun.

"Run along now, girls, before it gets too late."

Anna rode behind Mina on Tucan. It was almost a mile to the Hesslers, and they headed away from the creek, up through the mesquite trees. The sun was already halfway to the horizon.

Mina's heart began to pump rapidly as they neared

the cabin. They skirted around the plowed-up barren garden. Daniel and his father looked up from chopping wood as the girls approached, and waved. How strong he looked with his shirt sleeves rolled up showing his muscular brown arms, Mina thought.

He lay down the axe, and came over to take Tucan's reins and tie him up.

"*Guten Tag*, Mina, Anna. What brings you?"

Mina slid off Tucan, flipped her braids behind her shoulders, and handed Daniel the cookies tied up in a cloth. "Oh, I made cookies, and I thought your family might like some."

When Daniel smiled it made Mina feel slightly limp. His whole face became radiant under his yellow shock of hair, and his blue eyes seemed to know too much about her thoughts. She found herself staring rather dumbly, overwhelmed by the golden looks of him.

"*Danke*. I didn't know you were a cook."

Mina could think of nothing to say, and she stammered — something she had never done before — "Sh . . . sh . . . sure, I *love* to cook."

It was a lie. Actually she hated to cook or mend or any of those womanly things. She would much rather be out riding Tucan or going with Papa on his hauling trips. Well, she couldn't tell that to Daniel. What would he think of her?

"Papa says I'm a very good cook," Mina lied.

Anna put her hand over her mouth and giggled. Mina shot an angry look at her.

Frau Hessler came out of the cabin toward them with little Willie tagging along behind her. She was a stout blonde woman — always cheerful. Daniel handed her the cookies.

"*Guten Tag*, girls." She opened the cloth and looked at the golden cookies. "Well, bless you and your mama." She gave both of them a hug. "You come on in and sit by the fire for a few minutes. I have some coffee brewing." Turning to her husband she said, "Come along now,

Emil, we will have some coffee and cookies, and then you and Daniel can finish your work before dark."

Mina followed *Frau* Hessler toward the cabin. She stole a quick look at Daniel and caught him looking at her. She smiled and looked away.

Inside, the cabin was dark, but a cheery fire burned on the hearth. They talked about Papa and when he would return, and about baby Peter. Mina heard herself talking, but all the time she felt Daniel's gaze upon her, and wondered what he was thinking. Did he like her?

"Well, it's getting late, and we have work to finish, Daniel." *Herr* Hessler got up and started for the door.

Daniel held Tucan as Mina climbed on, and then he helped Anna get up behind her. Both girls waved as they left the Hesslers' cabin. It seemed to Mina that Daniel's eyes were only on her, and they looked sad as he waved back.

"He likes you, Mina," Anna whispered.

"Ja, ja, ja, ja," Mina sang softly in the melody of the German song she knew so well. Tucan turned his head to the side to see what was wrong with his mistress.

"Tucan thinks you're crazy, too." Anna giggled. They were quiet for a moment, and Anna continued. "There is no one for me. I'll be an old maid."

Mina turned so she could see Anna's face. She was pouting with her dainty lips pursed.

"I know, Anna, we'll find you an Indian warrior."

"Ohhhhhhh," Anna screamed.

Tucan jumped, startled.

"Anna, you musn't scream when you're riding a horse." Mina stroked Tucan's neck. "Don't worry, Tucan, it's only my silly friend, Anna. She didn't mean to frighten you."

Anna put her head against Mina's back, and they began to giggle again. All the tenseness went out of Mina, and she relaxed and let Tucan carry her along.

The sun was getting low, and Mina knew *Tante* Lisette would start worrying about her. At the Kaufmanns' cabin Anna slid off, and Mina waved goodbye. She was anxious to get home, but she wished Papa would be there to welcome her.

As Mina rode up the bank to the cabin she heard an owl hoot. It sent shivers through her body, and her heart began to pound wildly. Almost without realizing it, Mina began to hum. There was something frightening about the hooting. Then it came again from over in the under-brush along the road. Was it a Comanche?

Mina started singing. Indians are said to believe that singers are protected by the Great Spirit. She sang softly at first and then louder and louder.

Du, du liegst mir im Herzen,
Du, du liegst mir im Sinn.

By the time she got to the part, *Ja, ja, ja, ja,* she was al-most shouting. Tucan turned around to look at her.

The hooting came again as Mina dismounted, and Tucan shied and shook his bridle to be rid of it.

"Come, Tucan, I'm going to tie you up tonight." Mina led him around to the back of the cabin and with shaking hands tied him to the washing tree.

She wanted to run but made herself walk to the cabin, singing so everyone could hear.

Lisette opened the door and let her in. Mina quickly bolted the door behind them.

12

COMANCHE TROUBLE

"Mina, what is it?" Lisette asked, a frightened expression on her face.

Mina knew she had to keep calm. Papa had given her the duty of firing the shotgun if need be, and she must keep a level head and a steady hand.

She took a deep breath and then answered, "Oh, I heard an owl down by the road, and it sounded odd."

"Odd?"

"*Ja*, like it was not really an owl."

"Like what?"

Mina didn't say. She got Papa's shotgun down from over the door, and went to a place on the wall where she removed a loose stone in the chinking. It left a hole big enough for the double barrels of the gun and a view to the front of the cabin.

Mina poked the barrel through and pressed her face up to the hole. There was still some light left in the sky — just enough to make silhouettes of the trees. Mina watched. Suddenly Tucan whinnied, and Peter began to cry. Lisette picked him up and began to bounce him nervously.

"There's someone out there, *Tante* Lisette, I feel it."

"If only Ernst was here," Lisette said, bouncing Peter more vigorously.

The shotgun was loaded and ready to fire. Papa always left it that way. Mina pulled the hammer back with her thumb to full cock, and put her finger on the front trigger. She steadied the barrel on the wall, for she was beginning to tremble.

Tucan whinnied again. Mina watched through the hole, scanning from left to right, and then her eyes stopped at the live oak. There was a bump on the right side of the trunk she had never noticed before. Her eyes were intent on that bump. Suddenly it moved, and she heard the owl hoot again. The bump stepped away from the tree. It was an Indian!

Her finger squeezed the trigger. There was a little flash and *Blough!* came the explosion. Smoke blotted out her sight of the Indian, and some of it seeped back in through the hole, choking her with its rotten smell. She cocked the second hammer, closed her eyes, and pulled the other trigger. *Blough!* Mina pulled the barrel back out of the wall. It was still smoking. She put her face up to the hole.

Peter was screaming and crying, frightened by the loud explosions.

"Peter, Peter," Lisette tried to soothe him, absently.

The smoke began to clear, but it was too dark now to see anything. Mina replaced the chinking, and turned to look at Lisette. The alarm on her face showed in the flickering light from the fireplace. She patted Peter, but he seemed to sense the danger.

"The men will come now, Mina, but you must reload the gun."

Mina fetched the powder horn and the leather bag of shot. She was glad to have something to do other than just wait for help to come. She stood the gun on its stock

53

and poured a measure of powder down each barrel. Her hand was shaking. She stuffed wads of cloth into the barrels and used the ramrod to poke them down. Finally she poured in some shot with a small horn dipper and rammed in another wad. It was ready to fire again.

Mina noticed her knees felt a little shaky, so she pulled up a chair and sat down facing the door with the gun in her hands.

Peter had stopped crying at last, and his eyes drooped as he lay his head on Lisette's shoulder and sucked his thumb. It was quiet.

Had she killed the Indian? Or was he skulking around the cabin this very minute, looking for a way to get in. Mina shuddered.

"We must pray, Mina."

"You pray, *Tante* Lisette, and I'll keep watch." Mina had no patience with praying at a time like this. Papa always said, "God helps those who help themselves." And Mina intended to give God all the help He needed. *Tante* Lisette could do the praying.

"Our God in heaven . . ." she murmured, and Mina stopped listening to the words. She focused on the door. It was a solid wooden door, securely bolted, and yet . . .

There was a scraping noise just outside the door that set her heart pounding. Mina had heard stories of Comanches kidnapping young girls. One of them had escaped and returned to Fredericksburg, bruised and dirty, one ear cut off, hair stringing down, and a vacant look in her eyes.

When Lisette finished, Mina went to the door and listened. She heard distant hoofbeats. "They're coming!"

The sound of hoofbeats got louder and closer until the sound stopped just outside. Someone shouted, "Ho," and suddenly there was banging on the door. "Lisette, Mina, are you in there?" It was *Herr* Hessler.

Mina quickly unbolted the door. There stood *Herr* Hessler, Daniel, and *Herr* Kaufmann, who held a blazing torch.

"What is it? What happened?" they asked all at once.

"An Indian," Mina blurted out. "There was an Indian right over there by the oak tree. I saw him."

"Come on, let's have a look," *Herr* Kaufmann said, and the three men walked cautiously over to the tree with guns ready. They searched all around the cabin, but found nothing.

"Well, Mina, I think you scared that Indian away. It was probably a Comanche looking to steal Tucan," *Herr* Kaufmann said.

"Come in, come in," Lisette invited.

Herr Hessler suggested that Daniel could stay to protect them in case the Indians returned. "I believe they are gone, Lisette. Still, with Ernst away, it would be wise to have a man in the house."

Daniel smiled, "Sure, I'm happy to stay and keep watch."

Later that night after the men had gone, Mina climbed the ladder to her loft. From her bed she could see Daniel sitting before the fire staring into its embers, his gun across his knees. She felt safe again. It was almost as good as having Papa there. But *when* was Papa ever going to return?

13

A LETTER FROM GERMANY

Outside, the north wind buffeted the cabin and howled angrily as it was forced to go around the sturdy log walls. Inside, a lively fire flickered on the hearth.

Mina sat crosslegged on a braided rug before the fire watching Peter as he tried to get up on all fours.

"Come, Peter," she urged, "come to me."

Peter looked at her, gurgled, and moved one arm forward, then one knee, the other arm, the other knee. When he reached her, she picked him up and lifted him high. His cheeks, all plump and ruddy, glowed in the firelight as he laughed with delight.

"Papa will not believe how you have grown, baby Peter." Mina sighed. She always thought of Papa at this time of day and wished for him the most when darkness was coming.

Lisette sat in her chair by the fire making a long braid of rags to enlarge the hearth rug.

Presently the wind died down, and all was quiet except for the sizzling fire and the clock ticking. Mina heard the rumbling of a wagon down on the road.

"It's Papa!" Mina put Peter back down on the rug, and his eyes followed her as she ran to the door and flung it open.

Soft flakes of snow floated down from the darkening sky. Mina stepped out into the shaft of doorlight, and there was Papa walking alongside the wagon. Tucan whinnied nervously.

"Papa!" Mina ran toward him through the veil of snow.

He stopped with his arms open to her as he always did, and she flew into them, captured once again in his safe embrace. How good it felt. The damp snow fell on her neck and melted down her back, but she didn't care. Papa was home, and she liked his rough beard against her cheek.

"How is my *kleine* Mina?"

She stepped back and looked at Papa's face. He smiled at her but his eyes remained sad.

"Are you tired, Papa? Have you come a long way today?"

"*Jawohl*, Mina, all the way from Fredericksburg. I started before dawn."

"Ernst!" Lisette came running from the open door, and Papa clasped her tightly to him for a moment without speaking.

"But we'll all catch cold standing out here in the snow," Lisette said. "And I must see to Peter."

"*Ja, ja*, Lisette, I'll come just as soon as I take care of the oxen. You go on in."

The snow began to fall more thickly until Mina had to blink it off her eyelashes. They hurried to unhitch the oxen, and at last came in to the warm fire. Peter squealed in delight as Papa held him up high over his head.

"So . . ." Papa began as he took off his coat and hung it up on the peg, "how did it go while I was away? Did anything happen?"

Lisette and Mina looked at each other, and both started laughing.

"Did something funny happen?"

"Well, we had a visitor, Ernst," Lisette answered.

"A Comanche," Mina blurted out and felt a tremor through her body at the sound of the word.

Papa's expression froze. He watched Mina, and listened to her tell how she had seen the Indian behind the tree, how she had fired and reloaded the gun, and how the neighbors came.

Papa nodded his head thoughtfully. "Well, I couldn't have done better myself. I'm proud of you both, especially my *kleine* Mina." He put his arm around her shoulders and gave her a hug.

Then he pulled a letter from the inside pocket of his coat, and carefully opened it. "This came to the *Verein* headquarters in New Braunfels."

"Oh, a letter, a letter," Mina cried, jumping up and down. "Is it from *Opa*? Is it, Papa?"

Papa's eyes were sad as he looked at Mina, so vibrant before his eyes.

"*Nein*, Mina, it's from your cousin Christine."

Somehow, the way Papa said it, dropping his voice at the end, sent a pang of fear through her body. She didn't want to ask, but she had to.

"What's wrong, Papa?"

"Let me read it to you." And he began:

Wehrstedt, Germany
January 21, 1847

My dearly beloved Uncle Ernst, Aunt Minchen,
and Mina,

I wonder where you are, what kind of home and village you have. Time passes on, and we have no word from you.

Alas, with time comes change, and I have the sad duty to tell you that Opa is gone. He caught cold this winter, and it went into pneumonia. Somehow he was

59

never the same after you left. It was as though his heart broke. I miss him terribly.

Mina's throat grew tighter and tighter, and tears rolled freely down her cheeks as she thought of the last time she had seen *Opa*. He had been standing on the dock at Linden, as their riverboat pulled away. She saw tears glistening in his eyes and brimming over to run down his cheeks and hide in his grizzled beard. His sad, big eyes were just like Papa's, wide-set in his broad face. He raised his arm to wave at them as the boat rounded a bend in the river and then she could see him no longer. Never . . . never again would she look into his face.

Papa continued reading, but his voice had lost its steadiness.

I miss you too. The house, and my room in particular, seem empty and quiet without you, Mina. Why cannot our lives stay like they were? Why must everything change? Even Hans wants to go to America when he grows up, and will talk of nothing else.

Little Hans! Mina remembered how he had chased after the wagon as they rode out of the village. Finally he was left behind, and he stood waving his short arms violently until the wagon rounded a curve in the road, and he was lost from sight.

Their village of Wehrstedt, nestled in the valley, was soon farther and farther behind them, until it was like someone else's village, in a painting.

So much had happened since then. Christine didn't even know Mama was dead. Now *Opa* was dead. There was no going back to the village, to being *Opa's kleine* Mina ever again. Why *must* everything change, Mina wondered.

Papa continued:

I know I shall never go to Texas. I could not stand to leave all that is familiar, or the frightening voyage across the sea. But you are different, Uncle Ernst. You are strong and brave.

We have a new village schoolmaster, as *Herr* Bremer has also gone to Texas. *Herr* Schuessler is his name — from Berlin. He thinks I should go on to the *Gymnasium* in Bad Salzdetfurth, and study to be a governess. I rather like the idea.

Please write and tell us all about your life in Texas.

With kindest regards,
Your niece, Christine

Papa looked up at Mina with his sad eyes. At that moment she wished they were back in Wehrstedt. Mama would be alive and beautiful. *Opa* might be alive because they were there . . .

"Mina, come, let's unload the wagon. I have brought some surprises." Papa took her hand, and together they started out to the wagon.

"Here, Ernst, the lantern." Lisette handed it to him, and closed the cabin door as they left.

14

A WAGON FULL OF TREASURES

The snow had stopped falling and lay soft on the ground. Papa set the lantern on the wagon seat as he began to pull back the heavy canvas cover, and shook the snow from it.

"Mina, there will always be changes. Everything that is alive must grow and change."

"And die," Mina said bitterly.

"*Ja*, and die. You're right. Some live long and useful lives, others are taken in their youth, as God wills it. Our duty to God is to live our lives to the best of our abilities — to live fully while we are on earth, and not to waste our time. That is what *Opa* would want us to do. We can't look back at what *was*, or could have been. We must look forward, and work hard for what is and *will* be."

Papa finished uncovering the wagon, and Mina gasped as she saw what he had brought from San Antonio. There were sacks of cornmeal, even some wheat flour, sugar, coffee, a plowshare and other tools, packages of seed, three bolts of colorful calico, and a Mexican saddle for Tucan.

Suddenly there came a frantic mewing from the front of the wagon.

"Oh, Papa! did you bring us a kitten?" Mina began to bounce up and down on her toes.

Papa said nothing but reached one hand down into the very bottom of the wagon and pulled out a furry striped kitten — all gray and black — and handed it to Mina.

She cradled the kitten in her arms, and it began to purr.

"Shall we name it Schnurri, Papa?"

"Of course." Papa patted her shoulder. "So, you see, Mina, life goes on." Then he reached down into the wagon again, brought out a little leather bound book, and handed it to her. "Here, a special present for you."

On the front was written My Journal, in gold, and all around was a border of flowers and leaves in gold also.

"How beautiful!" Mina opened the book and inside were blank parchment pages waiting to be written upon with pen and ink. "My very own journal!" She kissed him on the cheek, and then looked into his face. "You are always so wise, Papa. Will I ever be able to understand things for myself the way you do?"

Papa chuckled. After a moment of thought he said, "You see, Mina, that is called growing up. Each day we have a chance to learn. If you attend carefully and mark life well you will become wiser, probably wiser even than your Papa!" He chuckled again. "Now, here, let's carry these sacks into the cabin for tonight. The rest we will unload tomorrow or take to the Kaufmanns and Hesslers."

Before bedtime Papa read aloud from the big family *Bible*. Mina could not think about the words — only how safe the cabin felt with him inside, and the sound of his deep, soothing voice. The wind could rage, Comanches could creep near, but Papa was home, and all was well again.

It was quite late when Mina sat at her table and opened her new journal to the first page. Schnurri had already made herself at home, curled up on Mina's bed. Mina dipped the quill into the bottle and wrote:

The Journal of

Johanne Ernestine Wilhelmine Jordan

She formed each letter carefully, adding extra curlicues on the initial letters as *Tante* Lisette had taught her. Mina looked with satisfaction at the finished title page. Then beneath her name she added:

(Mina for Short)

On the second page she began:

February 18, 1848

Papa came home at last with a wagon load of supplies, a kitten which I have named Schnurri, and this journal. My heart nearly burst with joy to see him.

But he brought some sad news in a letter from cousin Christine. She wrote that Opa died. I can scarcely believe he is gone. Time changes everything.

Some changes are bitter, and some are sweet, and some are both. The changes in me are bittersweet, as I am becoming a young woman. Some days I want to stay a child, but more often I want to grow up. I think I love Daniel Hessler, and I hope he loves me. Perhaps staying the same would be very dull after all.

Mina blew out the candle and crawled into bed. The stone Lisette had heated by the fire warmed the bed, and Mina nestled down to sleep.

Papa climbed the ladder and poked his head through the loft opening.

"Are you still awake?" Papa asked in a loud whisper.

"*Ja*, Papa."

"Well, after all the news and talk, I forgot to say that three more families are coming to settle near Willow Creek."

"Who are they? Anyone we know?"

"*Ja*, all from Fredericksburg — the Mannheims, the von Trappes, and Karl Basse's family. Also we decided to engage a schoolteacher to come after spring planting — a *Herr* Lange from San Antonio. He speaks English and Spanish and he was a student at the University of Berlin."

Mina got up, went over to the loft opening, knelt and wrapped her arms around her father.

"I'm so glad, Papa."

"Goodnight, *kleine* Mina. Now get back in bed before you take a chill."

15

SCHOOL AGAIN

Mina parted and braided her hair more carefully than usual, and pulled on the yellow calico dress *Tante* Lisette made last year. It was a little short now, Mina thought, as she looked down at her sunbrowned legs and bare feet. Papa said she was growing like a weed.

When Anna arrived, they got on Tucan and started off for the first day of Willow Creek School. Of course, there was no schoolhouse yet, but the men had made split log benches and set them under the big live oak tree that marked the Jordan's property. Daniel carved the name on a rough board and hung it from the branches. Later the sign would go over the door. Now, the teacher, *Herr* Karl Friedrich Lange, had arrived.

Schnurri darted about underfoot like a wildcat and squawked when Tucan's hoof caught her on the side and sent her rolling into a little fur ball.

Papa straightened up and waved to them from the vegetable garden where he was chopping weeds which had grown, unwanted, in the sandy soil. It had been a wet spring that ended the drought. Bluebonnets covered the open meadows, and quail called, *Bob white, bob white.*

Tucan followed the trail along Willow Creek as Mina held the reins in one hand and her dinner pail in the other. The willow trees on its banks were lacy green, and even the pecan trees were putting out small clusters of leaves.

"What do you think of *Herr* Lange?" Anna asked shyly.

"Well, I've only seen him once — on his way to the Hesslers' last week. Seems quite a gentleman though, and handsome too. Papa says he's a real scholar."

"Ja," Anna sighed, "a perfect gentleman."

Mina turned around and looked at Anna. She had a dreamy expression on her face.

"Anna, he's too old for you!"

"I know it, but that doesn't keep me from admiring him. He's so . . . so dashing." Anna sighed again.

"Daniel told me he carries a revolver," Mina said.

"Really?"

Mina nodded.

As they neared the big live oak, several children were already sitting on the benches, and *Herr* Lange was standing tall and erect before them in his long black coat.

The girls dismounted. Mina removed the bridle, hobbled Tucan, and left him to graze on the spring grass. She knew he couldn't wander far and would come when she called.

Little Willie Hessler sat on one side of the front row and Elisa von Trappe on the other, her blonde hair rippled and curled down her back. The older children took the back rows, girls on one side, boys on the other, including Daniel who had come early with *Herr* Lange.

"Good morning, young ladies," *Herr* Lange greeted them in English, and bowed slightly from the waist.

"Good morning, *Herr* Lange," Mina and Anna replied, and Anna even attempted a curtsy. Mina thought she looked ridiculous trying to be such a lady with bare feet.

"You silly goose," Mina whispered after they sat down.

Anna shot a cross look back at her. But, since they were not supposed to talk or even whisper, she said nothing.

Herr Lange greeted the children as they arrived. Then he counted them, pointing at each.

"So, all ten are here now, and we can begin," he said. "Let's bow our heads . . . Heavenly Father, bless this gathering of children and youths and make them eager to learn the wisdom of Thy world. Amen."

Once again all eyes were on *Herr* Lange. While his features were sharp, his eyebrows were thick and dark, and Mina noticed he could raise the left one without raising the other. She tried but could not do it.

"How many of you have books?"

Papa had bought a *McGuffey Third Reader* for Mina on his trip to San Antonio, and she held up her hand. Anna had *Webster's Speller*. Both had their slates from Germany.

"So, we'll start with reading. Mina and Anna will share a reader, and I have one here for you, Daniel."

After *Herr* Lange had arranged for all to have books he said, "While I hear Elisa and Willie, the rest of you are to study and prepare your reading lesson."

Mina opened her book to the first lesson and offered the right side of the book to Anna. At the beginning of Lesson One, "The Shepherd Boy," was a drawing of a young child sitting in a highchair with some playthings spread out on the table. His mother is about to pick him up.

Before beginning to read, Mina leaned forward slightly to look at Daniel at the other end of the bench. She had never seen him with his hair parted and plastered down neatly and his shirt collar buttoned up tightly around his neck. Daniel glanced up and caught Mina looking. She felt the blood rush to her face as she returned to her reader again.

Anna was ready to turn the page and nudged Mina to finish. As Mina read she could hear Tucan and Daniel's horse chomping contentedly as they moved slowly away from the live oak to find more grass. Occasionally one of them would shake his head and snort, happy to be rid of the bridle.

Elisa and Willie recited the English alphabet together as *Herr* Lange listened and prompted when they faltered.

When it was Mina's turn to read aloud, she and Anna went forward and sat on the reciting bench before *Herr* Lange.

"Will you read first, Mina?"

She sat up straight, flipped one braid back of her shoulder, and began . . .

The Shepherd Boy

Little Roy led his sheep down to pasture,
And his cows, by the side of the brook:
But his cows never drank any water,
And his sheep never needed a crook.

It was a story about a small boy pretending to be a shepherd with white pebbles for sheep and a ribbon for the brook.

"You read English very well, Mina," the teacher said when she had finished, and his left eyebrow raised itself.

"Thank you, *Herr* Lange."

At noon Mina and Anna took their dinner pails and sat down on a tree root overlooking Willow Creek. *Herr* Lange, Daniel, and Willie ate their dinner on the school benches. Some of the younger children slid down the bank, crossed the sandy bed, and waded in the shallow water.

As Mina watched, little Elisa slipped and dropped her dinner pail into the creek. At once she began to cry, her eyes clenched shut as the water ran over her bare feet.

Herr Lange and Daniel came quickly to where Mina and Anna sat. "Never mind, Elisa," the teacher called, "I'll share my dinner with you."

She stopped crying a moment and looked up at him, then back at her fallen dinner. A piece of yellow corn bread was carried along down the creek. She watched it and began to cry again.

Anna stood and quickly climbed down the embankment. When she reached Elisa, she took the corner of her apron and wiped away the tears.

Suddenly Tucan whinnied, and in that instant Mina realized she had not seen her horse for quite some time. Now her heart leaped in alarm though she was not sure why.

16

VISITORS

Mina looked around. The horses were nowhere in sight. Where had they wandered?

Daniel turned and ran back to the live oak at the edge of the open meadow where they had left the horses to graze. Mina was right behind him.

Another whinny. Mina looked to the left, and there beyond the meadow two Indians — Comanches? — were struggling to lead the horses away. They had ropes around the necks of the horses, but Tucan was rearing up and threatening the Indian with his forelegs.

Mina caught her breath. Then she let it out in a scream, *"Tucan!"* Without thinking she began to run toward them. "Tucan!"

The horse jerked his head up, pulling the rope out of the Indian's hands. The rope flew about and the Indian grabbed at it. Suddenly Tucan bolted away from him.

Mina felt a hand on her right arm, stopping her, holding her back.

"Mina, stop!" It was *Herr* Lange.

71

Daniel took hold of her other arm.

In front of them some twenty feet the Comanche stood for an instant like a statue, his greased body shining in the sun. The other Indian was struggling to get control of Daniel's horse who was backing off.

Mina turned and looked at *Herr* Lange. In his outstretched arm he held the revolver pointed at the Indian. He let go of Mina and steadied the pistol with his other hand and aimed carefully.

Crack! The shot ripped the air, and the Comanche grabbed his shoulder, turned and fled into the bushy undergrowth and over a rise.

Daniel's horse broke free. *Herr* Lange fired again, this time at the other Indian who ducked and was gone.

Daniel let go of Mina's arm and began running after the two Comanches.

"Stop, Daniel, don't follow them," *Herr* Lange shouted.

But Daniel paid no heed, and kept on running. *Herr* Lange pointed his pistol straight up in the air and fired a third time. Daniel stopped and looked around.

"Come back, I say, Daniel. They only wanted the horses, not a war. Let them go."

Mina's heart was pounding. She stood unmoving, trying to understand what had happened.

Reluctantly Daniel started back, looking down at the ground. Mina thought he was pouting. Then he stopped, pointing at a flat rock.

"Look, *Herr* Lange, you hit him. There's blood on this rock."

Sure enough, there were three drops of dark red blood on the rock and more on the grass.

Herr Lange looked at his pistol, blew on the barrel, and stuck it back inside his belt.

"Well, we sure scared them off, didn't we?" *Herr* Lange chuckled a bit nervously. He adjusted his coat and seemed to assemble his thoughts.

Mina looked around for Tucan. There he was with

Daniel's horse near the live oak, his eyes wild, ready to bolt again. She approached him slowly, stroked his neck, and talked softly in his ear. When he turned to look at her, the wildness had gone out of his eyes.

Anna comforted little Elisa who was sobbing, "I want . . . to go . . . hommmmme."

Herr Lange knelt down in front of Elisa. "Of course you do. It's all right. The Comanches have gone and they won't be back." He dried her eyes with his handkerchief. "I'll take you home myself."

Then the teacher stood to his full dark height, raised one eyebrow and, with dignity, announced, "School is out for today."

Something broke loose inside Mina and even in the little children who had huddled around *Herr* Lange. They began to jump up and down, clapping their hands, and squealing, "School is out!" They joined hands and began to circle around the teacher chanting, "School is out, school is out."

Herr Lange looked at them, disbelief in his eyes that his wards could change from a huddled, fearful group into this dancing circle.

Then he held up his hand for silence and waited until the last movement was stilled. "Now, go home and tell your fathers to meet here this evening at four o'clock. We're not going to let a couple of Comanches stop us from having school. No indeed!"

17

OLD FRIENDS

Together, all the families decided the time had come to talk to Chief Custaleta and form an alliance with the Lipans against the Comanches. Fortunately, *Herr* Lange could speak Spanish, which the Lipans understood.

After supper when Mina said to Papa, "May I go too?" he nodded his head thoughtfully and answered, "*Ja*, Mina, since you are a friend of the Chief and his daughter, you could be a real help."

Mina stood before Papa hardly daring to believe what he said. Her mouth fell open.

Papa laughed heartily. "At last my *kleine* Mina gets to go on an adventure with the men!" He took a puff on his pipe and enjoyed her amazement.

"Oh, Papa, do you really mean it?" She knew he did, for Papa was not one to tease. Mina began to dance around him.

Peter watched her from Lisette's knee, and squealed with delight. Mina picked him up and danced, holding him in her arms.

"Do you know, Peter, that your big sister is going to visit an Indian chief?"

Peter laughed with her, and she whirled around and around.

"You'll make him lose his supper, Mina," *Tante* Lisette warned, but she was smiling at the two of them.

Early the next morning five of the men, including Daniel, arrived and together they rode on to the von Trappe and Mannheim cabins downstream toward the Llano River. Mina rode behind Papa on Tucan, and the shotgun lay across the front of the saddle. Mina had on her blue beaded belt Custaleta had traded her for the locks of golden hair. In her pocket she carried a string of glass beads as a gift for him.

Going with Papa was something Mina had longed to do, had begged to do. Now here she was, one girl with seven men, on an important mission — yes, an adventure. To her surprise she felt strange, as though she didn't quite belong.

So Mina was quiet, listening and thinking as she rocked along behind Papa. The men talked of newborn calves, and how the soil was not made for farming. It was too shallow and rocky and often dry. Daniel was being one of the men as he rode along carrying an iron barrel hoop, for making arrow points, as another gift to Custaleta.

When they neared the Llano River, the talk turned to Indians.

"You're sure these Lipans are friendly, Ernst?" *Herr* Mannheim asked.

"*Ja*, I'm sure," Papa said nodding his head. "Mina will see to that."

"Oh, Papa," she whispered.

"No, I mean it." Turning, he pointed at her waist. "See, she wears a belt that belonged to the Chief's daughter."

At the Llano River they turned east and followed its grassy banks until the tepees of Custaleta's encampment came into sight. They reined in the horses and studied the camp for a moment. Some twenty tepees were clustered alongside the river, and smoke was rising from many of them.

From the cluster came a group of Lipans, perhaps a dozen, riding to meet them. Stopping a short distance away, three of them — one was Custaleta himself — dismounted and stood proud and erect.

Papa, Mina, and *Herr* Lange dismounted also, and Papa took Mina by the hand.

"Come, you must call Custaleta by name so he will know us." Papa raised his right arm in the peace signal, and the three began to walk toward the Chief.

Custaleta watched them approach, his face like stone with a slash of red paint across his cheekbones and nose. Copper hoop earrings shone on his left ear. And there, interlaced in his long braid were Mina's golden locks.

"Chief Custaleta, it's Mi–na." Her heart pounded as she watched for a sign of recognition.

The young warriors, spears in hand, but not at the ready, watched them closely.

"Mi–na," she repeated.

Custaleta said some words to one of the warriors, but never took his eyes off the three of them.

Papa stopped and held Mina back a moment, waiting.

Custaleta slowly raised his right arm in a gesture of peace. Papa, Mina, and *Herr* Lange approached, and she clutched the beads tightly in her hand. When they stood face to face, Mina saw again the faint flicker of expression on Custaleta's immobile face. It was just something that passed across lashless eyes, nothing more.

Herr Lange spoke in Spanish some words they had rehearsed on the way.

"Great Chief Custaleta, we have come on the peace path to greet you as friends and join together to protect ourselves from the marauding Comanches. Will you allow us to enter your village and talk in your council lodge?"

Mina thrust the beads before him in her open moist palm. "For you, Chief Custaleta, a gift." The sun glinted on the blue and green faceted beads and caught his eye.

Custaleta took the string of beads and turned them back and forth watching the sun bounce from one facet to another. Then he looked back at *Herr* Lange and answered.

Herr Lange translated his words. "He says that the hearts of his people were alarmed to see so many strangers who had not previously announced their coming and whose intentions were unknown. But since we have declared our purpose, all is well."

Custaleta mounted his horse, and motioning all to follow, turned back toward his village and led the way.

18

AND NEW ENEMIES

"So, the Chief remembered you, Mina," *Herr* Lange said.

"I suppose so. It's hard to know what he's thinking." Mina looked at Daniel. He had a half smile on his face as though he had been studying her. Mina glanced away quickly.

As they approached the camp, women and children formed two lines to welcome the visitors. Mina and Papa led the way as the black-eyed children waved feathers at them and danced about.

Then a girl broke from the line and ran up to Mina.

"Mi–na — " she sang out, "A–ma–ya." She walked along beside Tucan, smiling up at Mina.

The lines led them to the Council Lodge which was surrounded by young warriors.

Mina slid off the horse and stood facing Amaya, who was a young woman now and prettier than Mina remembered. Her black hair was neatly combed back and hung in a single braid over her shoulder.

Mina took her hand. "A–ma–ya." She could say no more. Mina turned to *Herr* Lange in desperation.

"Tell her I'm very glad to see her again."

"Mina *dice que está muy alegre de verla otra vez.*"

Amaya smiled broadly and then spoke to *Herr* Lange in Spanish, pointing to a hill in the distance.

"Amaya says you have given her much happiness by your visit. She would like to know if you wish to ride together to the lookout point, while the men talk in the council lodge."

"Is it all right, Papa?"

"Very well, Mina, but don't go far, just the two of you."

As the men filed into the lodge, Mina wished that she could enter and just listen as they talked and smoked the long pipe. Daniel was last and paused a moment, glancing at her as he leaned over to enter.

"Daniel — don't get sick on the pipe."

He flashed his big smile at her and disappeared inside the lodge.

Amaya watched her, head cocked to one side. Then she led the way down to the river and they drank from their hands. Amaya pulled strips of jerky and some ash-cakes from a leather pouch and offered them to Mina. The jerky was tough and leathery, but Mina chewed on it hungrily. Small children tagged along until the girls mounted their horses — Amaya on her paint — and started off toward the lookout point.

They rode silently. It was strange, thought Mina, to be friends and unable to talk. The air between them seemed filled with unspoken words.

Finally Amaya broke the silence. "Dan–iel?" she asked and pointed to Mina.

Mina understood the question right away, shook her head no, and laughed. "No, Daniel not my husband." Then pointing at Amaya she asked, "You?"

"No," Amaya answered shaking her head from side to side.

They both laughed.

"Too–young–to–marry," Mina pronounced slowly.

"Tu yung?"

"*Si*, too young. But I like him."

Amaya looked at her quizzically.

Mina tried sign language. "Dan–iel," she said and patted her chest over her heart.

"Ah, *si*," Amaya said. Then she pointed to herself. "Chaco," and patted her chest as Mina had done.

"You like Chaco?"

"*Si*."

By this time they were nearing the hill.

"Let's race," Mina said and gestured ahead to Amaya. She nudged Tucan in the ribs with her heels, and he dashed away in a gallop.

The two girls raced for the hill. Mina's braids were flying as she gripped Tucan with her knees. She thought of *Tante* Lisette's words, "You ride like a wild Indian," and let herself be carried along. Amaya was beside her, leaning forward over her horse's neck. On and on they went, faster and faster. Mina clung to Tucan. She had never ridden so fast. Something wild seemed to happen to her horse, and startled, Mina realized she couldn't stop Tucan if she tried. Amaya fell behind and was shouting something. Mina pulled back on the reins. Up ahead there were people on horseback — Comanches!

Tucan stopped suddenly, reared up, and Mina felt herself falling. She hit the ground. Tucan's hoofs were dancing around near her head. Mina struggled up and stood, but everything was whirling around — there was Tucan, and two Indians. One of them reached from his horse and grabbed Tucan's reins. The other came riding at Mina.

She turned and ran screaming, "Get away, get away." Mina felt herself caught under the arms and lifted up on his horse as it ran. He sat her forcibly in front of him. Mina struggled to get loose, but the more she struggled the tighter he clamped his arm around her waist.

From the corner of her eye she saw Amaya. "Go for Papa," she yelled. Amaya turned quickly and galloped off in the direction from which they had come.

Heart pounding, Mina turned and looked at the face of her captor for an instant. It was a lean, cruel face, and the deep-set eyes glared fiercely at her as the Indian tightened his hold until she could hardly breathe.

19

A WILD RIDE

The Comanche guided the horse expertly, dodging a bush here, a rock there, finding the best way at full gallop. When they rode under a low branch, he pushed her down roughly, over the horse. They rode in silence. Up ahead Tucan was being led by the other Indian.

With the galloping gait of the horse, a word began to pound in Mina's head. Escape, escape, I must escape. Every second is taking me farther from Papa. He can't help me now.

The image of the vacant-eyed girl who had been captured by the Comanches flashed before her, and she shuddered. No, it musn't happen to me, Mina thought. I must escape.

Even in the tight grip of the Comanche a fierce will flooded over her, washing away the panic. She began to think clearly, searching for a way to break free of the Comanche's hold.

Suddenly it came to her — a daring plan which set her heart pounding anew. There was no time to consider

what might happen. Anything was better than being carried away. And she must do it *now — right NOW!* Mina gathered saliva in her mouth, turned, spit directly in the eyes of the Indian, and flung herself to the left with all her strength. He made a harsh sound, his arm gave way, and she began to fall headlong off the horse.

Just as she expected to hit the ground, she felt her ankle grasped and held tightly. The horse's hoofs pounded the ground at her face. Mina wrapped her arms around her head for protection as the horse kept on running, and she bounced against his flank. She was being dragged through bushes that scratched her arms and tore at her hair. She kicked the Comanche with her free leg, struggling to loosen his grip on her ankle.

Down an embankment, across a creek. Water splashed in her face. The horse scrambled up the other side as Mina reached out for something to hang onto. She caught hold of a branch. Her hands slipped along the bark, burning her palms, and her leg felt as if it were being torn from her body. Still, she clung onto the tree limb.

The horse stumbled for an instant, and Mina's leg was free. She rolled over and over, down to the creek.

At the top of the bank the Comanche wheeled his horse about and looked down at her with savage eyes. Yelling to his comrade, he jumped off his horse, pulled his knife, and started down the embankment.

Mina screamed and scrambled up the opposite bank on all fours. At the top she glanced back quickly. He was coming for her, knife held in his teeth, both hands ready. The other Indian, off his horse now, was struggling with Tucan who backed away and pulled at the reins.

"Tucan, come," she called and then turned and ran blindly, not knowing which way to go. Tucan whinnied again and again as though calling out to her. Strength surged through her body, and she ran like a wild thing. She listened for footsteps behind her, but all she could hear were her own, swishing through the tall grass.

Mina looked back and caught her breath. The Comanche was not there. Had he gone back for his horse? Would he come riding and snatch her up again?

There was a group of cedar trees ahead with thick lower branches, and Mina darted behind them. She was panting now, and blood pounded in her ears. But there was another pounding, coming closer and closer, the pounding of a horse's hoofs. He was coming for her. Mina crouched behind the thickest branches.

As the pounding neared she held her breath. *Tucan!* He came running wildly into the small clearing, reins flying. He stopped abruptly, pranced about and shook his head to be rid of the reins. Mina wanted to run out to him, but held herself back. She must not startle him. She must stay calm.

"Tucan," Mina called to him in a soft voice as she came slowly from behind the cedars.

He turned and looked at her, still for a moment. His eyes were wild.

"Tucan, let me ride you." She reached for the reins, noticing for the first time that her arms were bloody and the skin on her palms had been scraped raw. Mina looked at her outstretched hands and shuddered. It was almost as if she looked at someone else's hands — for she felt no pain.

Tucan jerked his head up, and appeared ready to dash off.

"Please, Tucan." She ran her hand along his neck, smearing blood on his black silky coat. Mina forced her voice to be soft and soothing, though her heart was racing. "Easy now, Tucan. You can save my life."

The skin on his neck quivered where her blood had been wiped. Slowly she picked up the reins and tied them over his neck. Her fingers were stiff and clumsy. Then with the back of her hand on the saddle horn she slipped her left foot in the stirrup, gave a jump, and they were off. Tucan bolted into a gallop while Mina was still struggling to get her leg over his back. With one final effort she was astride, and she let him carry her along. Tucan would take her back to Papa.

20

A LIPAN MAIDEN

Mina felt weak, almost limp. It was all she could do just to cling to the saddle and let Tucan have the reins. She felt as one with the horse — their will was the same, to escape the Comanches.

Her body rocked with his gallop until Tucan jolted to a stop. Mina looked around. They were at Lookout Mountain again, at the very place where she had been captured. Up ahead, there was a group on horseback. Tucan backed away, and seemed ready to bolt off in another direction.

There were Indians! There was — yes, it was Papa with Custaleta and Amaya, Daniel — all of them.

"Easy, Tucan," Mina took the reins then, and the little horse began to slow his pace.

When they met, Papa jumped off the horse he was riding and ran to Mina's side.

"Mina! *Thank God!* Are you all right? What have they done to you my *kleine* Mina?" He held up his arms to her.

Suddenly Mina felt shaky, and tears rolled down her cheeks. *"Oh, Papa!"* She couldn't say any more. She slid off Tucan into Papa's arms, his safe arms, where nothing could harm her. It was as if she were a little girl again, Papa's *kleine* Mina. She felt herself trembling. He hugged her and patted her back as the dam broke and sobs gushed forth.

"Now, now, my *kleine* Mina. Everything is all right. You are with Papa now."

When the sobs were over Papa held her out from him. His shirt was bloodied. He took her hands gently in his and examined them. Mina felt light-headed as she looked again at her scraped hands, and her knees were weak. Papa picked her up and carried her to the shade of an oak tree where Amaya had spread a blanket.

"We must stop the bleeding," Daniel said as he took off his shirt and began ripping it into strips.

Papa bandaged her arms with Daniel's shirt. Mina liked that, and after taking some sips of water that Papa held for her she felt better. She was *not* going to faint like a lady.

She smiled then at all the concerned faces. There was Papa on one side, Amaya on the other, and Daniel and the men gathered around. To her surprise a cheer went up. But Papa's expression did not change.

"Mina," he began, and hesitated as she looked at him. "Mina, did they . . . harm you?"

Mina felt herself blush as she realized what he meant.

"No, Papa, not in that way."

"Oh, thank God, thank God," Papa leaned over and hugged her again. "I would have killed them if they had harmed my *kleine* Mina."

"And I . . . I would have helped you, *Herr* Jordan," Daniel said boldly.

Mina looked at him. He stood barechested as an Indian, his yellow hair like the sun. He ducked his head and turned away, suddenly embarrassed at his own words.

"Thank you, Daniel, I appreciate that," Papa said.

Mina sat up, drank some more water, and watched as Custaleta dispatched four of his warriors in the direction the Comanches had gone. They galloped away whooping, urging on their spirited horses, and were out of sight in a moment. Then the chief spoke to *Herr* Lange in Spanish.

"Do you feel strong enough to go back to the village, Mina?" *Herr* Lange asked. "Chief Custaleta says the women will treat your wounds."

Mina looked at Amaya who nodded reassuringly.

So, with Papa and Amaya helping, Mina stood and walked to the horses. Her hands had begun to throb. For a moment she thought she might faint, but she drew a deep breath, and another.

"All right, Mina?" Papa asked.

She nodded yes with a little smile.

Daniel stood on the other side of Tucan in case Mina lost her balance as Papa helped her up. Papa got on behind her, and they started for the village.

Tucan was calm now. Papa held the reins with his arms on either side of Mina.

"Good, brave Tucan," Mina cooed to him. "You saved my life, Tucan." His slit ears twitched and he turned his head to look at her. "I would stroke you if I could." She rested her elbows on Papa's arms and looked at the bloody bandages. Held up like that they didn't throb so. "That's better," she said to Papa.

"Good, your color is returning too. We'll get the wounds cleaned and treated in the village and then take you home."

Mina did not like to think about having her hands and arms washed. It would sting, she knew, but there was no choice. She determined to endure it without flinching. Custaleta would like that. She would pretend that her hands did not belong to her.

"Tell me, Mina, how did you manage to escape?"

"Well, Papa, I knew if I didn't *do* something, I might end up like the girl who was kidnapped near Fredericksburg. Remember?"

Papa nodded his head.

"When I thought of her, it made me bold, and a plan came to my mind." Mina grew more animated as she talked, and the words came tumbling from her mouth.

When she finished the story, Papa shook his head in disbelief. "Not many girls would have acted so boldly, Mina. I thank God that you did. It could have been worse, much worse."

When they arrived at the village, Custaleta's wife, Wapako, and Amaya took over Mina's treatment. At the edge of the river they sat her down on a rock. Amaya pointed to the spiderwort blooming near the edge of the water. She wanted Mina to look at the blue flowers rather than at her hands as they gently removed the bandages. The two women, one on each side, poured water on her arms and hands. Mina caught her breath as she felt the water washing over her raw wounds. But she did not flinch. She looked at Wapako, a round-faced, still pretty woman who smiled approvingly at Mina and said, *"Muchacha valiente."*

The washing done, they let the sun dry Mina's arms. The scrapes on her hands and arms looked better with the blood and dirt washed away, but stung painfully. Wapako applied a paste made from prickly pear, and slowly the stinging was soothed.

"*Muchas gracias*, Wapako, Amaya," Mina said.

Wapako nodded and motioned Mina to follow her to her tepee. There she brought out a fringed doeskin dress, leggings, and moccasins for Mina to put on.

"*Porque tienes el valor de una doncella* Lipan," Wapako said.

Mina did not know what the words meant, but she understood that Wapako wanted her to wear the dress. Wapako and Amaya helped her out of her calico dress. The ruffle around the skirt had been torn and the sleeve ripped. The doeskin felt soft and supple on her body. Amaya refastened the beaded belt around Mina's waist, and undid the blonde braids. She removed the twigs and burrs that had caught there and carefully combed out Mina's long golden hair.

When they came out of the tent, Mina saw that the warriors had returned. Papa and the other men were watching as Custaleta heard their report. He spoke to *Herr* Lange. The Comanches had fled across many hills and valleys.

Papa spoke to Custaleta. He stood facing him as one chief to another and said, "We are proud to have you as friends and allies, Chief Custaleta. You and your people will always be welcome at Willow Creek."

As *Herr* Lange translated, Custaleta kept his steady eyes on Papa. Hearing the words, Custaleta came closer to Papa and they embraced and patted one another on the back.

Mina came and stood beside Papa.

"Look at my Lipan maiden!" he exclaimed. "Let's see your arms, Mina." Papa examined them carefully. "Well, they look much better. How do you feel?"

Mina nodded. "I'm all right, Papa." Turning to *Herr* Lange she repeated, as best she could remember, the

Spanish phrase Wapako had spoken, and asked what it meant.

"It translates that — you have the courage of a Lipan maiden."

Mina was pleased and she looked at Custaleta, searching for an expression of approval. He nodded his head once but his face remained immobile. Still, it was enough, and Mina understood. She had gained his respect. With this thought to help sooth her wounds, they started back to Willow Creek.

21

NEW FATHERLAND

It was early evening by the time they arrived at the first cabin, and *Herr* Mannheim turned off. Farther on, *Herr* von Trappe said farewell and splashed through the creek toward his cabin on the other side.

When they reached the big live oak, the sun was casting horizontal rays across the meadow of bluebonnets. Their perfume reached Mina's nostrils and she breathed in deeply. As they rode under the spreading branches a cardinal sang out, announcing his territory. Mina remembered when they first came to Willow Creek, Papa had stopped the wagon at this tree and said, *Now we are on our land.*

Our land. That was why they had left Germany and come to Texas — for land to call their own and a better life.

Many times Mina had longed to be back in *Opa's* big safe house in Wehrstedt. She remembered how she had clung tightly to *Opa* that morning they had left Wehrstedt, for good.

Now as she looked at this land — our land as far as she could see — she was glad they had come. They had, at last, found something better. How strange that she should feel glad after barely escaping with her life. It seemed to Mina that everything she saw and heard had become more vivid — the bluebonnets seemed bluer, the cardinal's song sweeter than she remembered.

Suddenly a vision of the Comanche's fierce face intruded into her thoughts, and she shuddered.

"Are you chilled, Mina?"

"No, Papa, just remembering the Comanche."

"You must try to forget."

"*Ja*, Papa, I will."

"He'll probably never forget the day he tried to kidnap a German girl of spirit," Papa said proudly.

After a few moments, Mina asked, "Papa, what do you think we would be doing if we were still back in Germany?"

Papa did not answer right away. The saddle squeaked as Tucan walked along with his slow rocking gait.

"It's hard to say, Mina. Perhaps we would have moved to Hamburg, so I could work in a textile mill."

"We wouldn't have land, would we?"

"No, nothing like this."

She turned for a moment — even though it pained her shoulder — and looked at Papa's broad face, his deep, sad eyes. "Well, thank you for bringing me to Texas."

"You still thank me after all that has happened?" He shook his head from side to side. "Sometimes I think we should never have come."

"No, Papa, that's not true. Oh, it was terrible at first. I wanted to go back home. When . . . when Mama died . . ." After all this time her throat still tightened at the thought.

She swallowed and went on. "I was afraid we might all die. It was you, Papa, who never gave up hope. And we survived, just as you said we would. Then, we found *Tante* Lisette and made this place for ourselves. All this is ours — every tree and rock and flower — our land, Papa."

"*Ja*, if only Mama could have lived to see this."

Mina agreed, nodding her head in silence.

"It was wrong to bring her," Papa continued. "She was never really strong. Somehow I thought the new country would give her strength and health. But it was not God's will."

They rode quietly for awhile listening to the sound of the horses' hoofs and the squeaking leather saddles.

Papa seemed to draw himself together, back from the past. "But you, Mina, it has made you stronger. Oh, you have always had fire in your veins." He chuckled. "Sometimes it got you into trouble, and I always feared that someone or something would put out the fire. Here in Texas that fire has burned even brighter." He paused. "You might even say it has forged a spirit of iron."

Mina liked Papa's words — *A spirit of iron*. She straightened in the saddle, feeling more alive than ever, even though her body was sore and scraped. She was aware of her heart beating, her blood coursing through her body. Today anything and all things were possible.

At the turning-off place Mina looked back at Daniel. He answered with a wave as he started across Willow Creek with his father and *Herr* Kaufmann.

She was glad the Hesslers had come to Texas too. Perhaps it was God's will that Mina and Daniel should meet. She was not sure. She *was* sure of *her* will, and that was to one day marry Daniel Hessler.

Mina and Papa passed the freshly plowed and planted garden. Smoke drifted up from the chimney, and Mina breathed in the smells of supper cooking — corn bread and sausage and coffee. They were home.

If Comanches came again, she and Papa would fight back. They would hold onto this place, this cabin, this beginning of a new fatherland with all their might for generation after generation. It would become like *Opa's* home place in Germany. Only here, there was enough land for everyone, sons and daughters alike.

96

GLOSSARY OF GERMAN WORDS

auf Wiedersehen	farewell, goodbye
danke	thanks
Frau	Mrs.
Fräulein	Miss, young lady
gute Nacht	goodnight
guten Tag	good day
Herr	Mr.
ja	yes
jawohl	yes indeed
kleine	little
nein	no
Tannenbaum	fir tree, Christmas tree
Tante	aunt
wie geht's	how are you
Weihnachts-baum	Christmas tree

borl   gh-
an e   om

       er
favc   il-
drei   ng
the   nd
Eur   he
Mid   he
spei   iey
wro   ers
and   ng

reac   iey
havi   rk.
The   ns.

Available from:
Eakin Press
1-800-880-8642